THE SHATTERED
PEACE

JEDI APPRENTICE

JEDI APPRENTICE

The Shattered Peace

Jude Watson

SCHOLASTIC INC.

New York Toronto London Auckland Sydney
Mexico City New Delhi Hong Kong

No part of this publication may be reproduced in whole or in part, or stored in a retrieval system or transmitted in any form or by any means, electronic, mechanical, photocopying, recording, or otherwise, without written permission of the publisher. For information regarding permission, write to Scholastic Inc., Attention: Permissions Department, 555 Broadway, New York, NY 10012.

ISBN 0-590-52084-9

12 11 10 9 8 7 6 5 4 3 2 1   0 1 2 3 4 5 6/0

Printed in the U.S.A.
First Scholastic printing, October 2000

THE SHATTERED PEACE

CHAPTER 1

Obi-Wan Kenobi peered through the dense cloud cover, hoping to catch a glimpse of the surface of the planet Rutan. All he saw was a thick gray mist that swirled around the starship, forming tiny droplets that trickled down the viewport.

He stretched out his legs impatiently. He was anxious to arrive on the planet and start the mission. It had been a long journey from Coruscant — his muscles felt cramped and he longed for fresh air. Their small starship, on loan from the Senate, had needed repairs, which had added a full day to their journey.

Noting his restless movement, his Master, Qui-Gon Jinn, glanced at him. "Control your impatience, Obi-Wan," he remarked. "The mission begins before it starts, when we can prepare for what lies ahead."

Obi-Wan suppressed a sigh. Qui-Gon was a Jedi Master, and his wisdom was legendary. His advice usually made sense after Obi-Wan thought about it a moment. But sometimes it could be difficult to follow. Especially when he had been sitting in a transport for three days, waiting to get somewhere.

Qui-Gon gave him a short smile. The good thing about Obi-Wan's Master was that even while he chided Obi-Wan's impatience, he understood it as well.

"So let us review what we know about the mission ahead," Qui-Gon suggested. "Information is preparation. What do we know about the history of Rutan and Senali?"

"Senali is an orbiting satellite of Rutan," Obi-Wan recited, remembering the information Jedi Master Yoda had provided them back on Coruscant. "Now it is a separate world with its own government, but it was a colony of Rutan for many years. The two worlds fought a long and difficult war that took its toll on both populations. The war was won by the satellite Senali in a surprising upset."

Obi-Wan stopped as his attention swerved and memory took over. Months ago, he had been involved in a civil war on the planet of Melida/Daan. In that conflict, the side with fewer weapons and lesser power had won, surprising not only the other side, but the galaxy. He knew firsthand how resolve and cunning could win out over superior forces.

"And what happened after that?" Qui-Gon prompted, breaking into his thoughts.

"Since the war was devastating to both worlds, a unique peace agreement was decided upon. The firstborn children of the rulers of both Rutan and Senali are exchanged when each child reaches seven years of age. The child is brought up on the neighboring planet, but is allowed to receive visitors and go for short visits to his or her home planet, as well as be in contact with the royal family. This is so that he or she does not forget his or her birth family or duty."

"And what happens when the child is sixteen?" Qui-Gon prompted.

"The child is allowed to return to his or her home planet in order to be groomed for leadership," the thirteen-year-old Padawan answered. "Another member of the ruling family takes his or her place until the next generation is born."

"It's an interesting solution to the problem of maintaining peace between two old enemies," Qui-Gon mused. "The thinking is that the leader of each world will not attack a planet where his or her child is residing. But the plan has a flaw that the rulers didn't take into account."

"What is that?" Obi-Wan asked.

"Feelings," Qui-Gon answered. "Loyalties are formed in your heart, not born in you. Emotion can't be ruled. Both leaders thought that if their children were with them for their first seven years, that would ensure their loyalty. But one can be loyal to one's home planet and yet want a different life."

"Like Prince Leed," Obi-Wan said. "He has lived on Senali for almost ten years. He does not want to return to Rutan."

Again, Obi-Wan thought back to his experience on Melida/Daan. He had wanted to join that society and live there. But even though he had made the choice to do so, he had not given up his loyalty to the Temple. Others had not seen it that way. He sensed that he would understand the torn feelings of Prince Leed.

"Or at least Leed *claims* he wants to stay on Senali," Qui-Gon amended. "That's what we're here to find out. His father believes the Senali are forcing him to stay. That's why the Senate fears that the two worlds will go to war again."

The mist began to break into patches of cloud. A large city appeared beneath them.

"That must be Testa, the capital city," Qui-Gon said. "The royal grounds of the king are on the outskirts."

Suddenly a warning light flashed on the control panel.

"I was afraid of this," Qui-Gon murmured. "Thanks to our detour, our fuel is very low."

He guided the craft closer to the planet's surface. They left the city behind and began to glide above a field of stubby, straw-colored grass. A warning alarm pinged.

"We're losing fuel fast. I can't make it to the royal landing platform," Qui-Gon said. He checked the coordinates. "If we land on this field, we won't be far from the palace. We're close enough to walk."

Obi-Wan flicked the controls that would prepare the ship for landing. Qui-Gon headed for level ground and guided the transport to a smooth stop.

"Let's just take our survival packs," Qui-Gon suggested. "No doubt King Frane will refuel the transport for us and we can fly it to the landing platform later."

Obi-Wan followed Qui-Gon down the ramp. Together they struck out across the field. Obi-Wan enjoyed the sensation of being outside again. He inhaled the fresh scent of the grass and tilted his head back to catch the faint rays of the sun that managed to filter through the clouds and mist.

Suddenly, Qui-Gon stopped. "Do you feel it?" he asked.

Obi-Wan felt nothing. But he waited before answering. Qui-Gon's perceptions were usually sharper than his. His Master had a deep connection to the Force that united all things.

Then he felt it, too — a vibration in the dirt beneath his feet.

"What is it?"

"I'm not sure," Qui-Gon said. He crouched and put a hand on the ground. "Not equipment. Animals."

Obi-Wan peered through the mist. Far away he thought he saw a cloud of dust rise from the field. The dry grass rippled, but there was no breeze. Then he picked out shapes through the mist. Galloping animals were heading toward them.

"They are running scared. It's a stampede," Qui-Gon said. He whipped his head around. "There's no time to find shelter, and we're too far from the trees. Run *with* them, Padawan. Do not let yourself fall or you'll get trampled."

"Run with what?" Now Obi-Wan could hear the pounding noise. "What are they?"

"Kudana," Qui-Gon said tersely. He scanned the air overhead. Dots that Obi-Wan had thought were birds suddenly dived and twisted like no birds Obi-Wan had ever seen. One of the dots zoomed toward them. It was a seeker droid. Obi-Wan saw an indicator light flash.

"A hunt," Qui-Gon corrected as in one smooth movement he withdrew his lightsaber and activated it. "And now we are the prey."

CHAPTER 2

The kudana rose out of the mist, the noise of their hooves like thunder. They were beautiful animals, their bronze metallic skins highly prized throughout the galaxy. Their eyes rolled in fright, and they made a high-pitched sound that was close to screaming. Obi-Wan could smell their panic, but he was more concerned about their sharp hooves and powerful legs.

The seeker droid hovered ahead, a laser beaming down toward Qui-Gon. No doubt it was sending back coordinates of their location.

"Ready, Obi-Wan?" Qui-Gon shouted over the noise. "Pick a kudana and run alongside it. Use the Force to reach out and connect. Then, if you can, ride one."

Obi-Wan began to run. Qui-Gon ran ahead of him, matching the animals' speed. He reached out to touch the nearest animal's flank, racing alongside it. Obi-Wan knew his Master was calling on the Force.

With a gigantic leap, Qui-Gon landed on the animal's back. While the animal bucked and twisted, trying to throw him, he slashed at the seeker droid with his lightsaber. Metal sizzled and the smoking droid fell to the grass. Qui-Gon leaned down and hugged the kudana's neck. It quieted, allowing him to ride.

Obi-Wan didn't see any of this. He was busy trying to avoid the flashing hooves of the kudana around him. Their panicked attempts to avoid the laser beams caused them to veer and swerve. He quickly saw that if the seeker droids weren't disabled, he would be trampled.

He, too, reached out gently to the animal closest to him, feeling its muscles bunch and quiver. He leaped high and landed on his feet on the animal's back. Quickly, he settled astride the animal, picking up the animal's rhythm so he would not fall. He reached out and connected with the frightened mind of the animal, sensing which way it would move.

Keeping his balance, Qui-Gon swung his lightsaber overhead at the next seeker droid. He slashed it in two pieces.

Obi-Wan held onto the silky mane of the kudana for a moment to get his balance, then leaped over the galloping animal to land on another. He swung his lightsaber as he jumped, and neatly cut another seeker droid in two.

The fourth seeker droid buzzed overhead, zooming forward to lock on Obi-Wan's position. Qui-Gon rode on a kudana by Obi-Wan's side, standing perfectly balanced and rocking with the movement of the animal's gait.

"I'll take care of it, Padawan!" he shouted. He reached up and demolished the seeker droid with a left-to-right swipe. Then he jumped off the kudana, keeping to the side of the pack. He motioned Obi-Wan to do the same.

Obi-Wan hit the ground and ran alongside the kudana. Now that they could not see the red lasers, the animals began to calm down. They ran easily, without the panic that had made them veer and shy. Gradually the animals surged ahead, and Obi-Wan found himself alone alongside Qui-Gon.

Qui-Gon slowed his stride and turned off his lightsaber. "Well, Padawan," he said, "my guess is that our mission has begun."

Obi-Wan tried to catch his breath. He felt the ground rumble underneath his feet once more. He and Qui-Gon turned at the same time. Clouds of dust rose in the distance.

"More kudana?" Obi-Wan asked.

"No," Qui-Gon said. "We have seen the prey. Now we'll meet the predators."

Soon Obi-Wan could distinguish creatures called huds coming from the distance. They were native to Rutan, four-legged creatures with black-and-red-striped coats, bred for their strength and speed. Blue-skinned Rutanians rode on their backs, dressed in colorful furs and hides. Barking alongside and occasionally leaping up to snap at the heels of a hud were fierce nek battle dogs attached to the huds' saddles with tethers. Despite their fierce, unpredictable natures, many Rutanians bred them and kept them as hunters and pets.

Qui-Gon waited as the group rode up to them. The Rutanian at the head of the party swung off his hud with an angry motion.

Rutanians were known for their height, standing nearly a meter taller than Qui-Gon. This Rutanian was taller than most. He was a hostile presence, dressed in the skin and pelts of various creatures sewn together with thick silver cord in a colorful patchwork. His long, glossy hair was elaborately braided and hung over his shoulders. His thick fingers, overgrown with hair, were covered with jeweled rings.

"You scared away my herd!" he bellowed, stomping toward the Jedi in heeled boots.

"Black holes and blast the galaxy! What kind of fools are you?"

"We are the Jedi you summoned from Coruscant, King Frane," Qui-Gon said calmly.

"You're a couple of gundark brains!" King Frane continued to bellow. "Did you see that herd — we could have captured twenty-five skins at least. I've been tracking them for three days. You'll pay for this!"

Obi-Wan looked at Qui-Gon to see how he would respond. He couldn't believe that King Frane had insulted the Jedi in such a rude fashion. Would Qui-Gon turn on his heel and leave?

Qui-Gon was silent for a moment. He stared at King Frane without rudeness, waiting out his anger. The intelligence and calm in the Jedi's gaze soon made King Frane uncomfortable. His unease quickly changed back to anger.

"Don't use any Jedi mind tricks on me!" he fumed. "You destroyed my sport for today. I've a mind to send you back to your Temple and declare war on the Senalis! At least I know I can blast them before they get away."

"Especially if you have seeker droids to track them," Qui-Gon said. "Aren't seeker droids illegal on Rutan? I understood that they were outlawed so all Rutanians would have an equal chance at the game. Even the king," Qui-Gon added pointedly.

King Frane's glassy green eyes glinted in his dark-blue skin. Obi-Wan could not decipher what he saw there. Would the king explode and insult them further? Obi-Wan knew that hunting was a popular pastime on Rutan. Rutanian skins and pelts were renowned throughout the galaxy for those who wore such things. Animals were bred specifically for the smoothness and beauty of their hides. Then they were sent in the wild in order to provide sport for the population.

King Frane prided himself on being the best hunter of all. Lists of kills were posted at the end of every year, and the king was always first. Now Qui-Gon had exposed the fact that he cheated.

Suddenly, King Frane let out a loud, explosive laugh. The royal party behind him broke out into nervous chuckles as well.

"Trumped by a Jedi! I'll be a gundark brain myself!" King Frane chortled. "I can see that I sent for the best minds in the galaxy. That means I am as smart as they are, am I not?"

He threw an amiable arm around Qui-Gon's shoulder. "Come, friend," he said. "I am glad to see you after all. You and your young companion are welcome to join us at our feast. There, we can discuss the foul and treacherous Senali."

CHAPTER 3

   The Jedi were led into a vast stone hall in the center of the royal palace. A huge bonfire was blazing in a pit set in the middle of the hall. The surrounding walls were blackened with smoke. Nek battle dogs lay on the cold stone floor, chained to posts carved with scenes of past battles. Stuffed heads of kudana and other native creatures were mounted on the walls at regularly spaced intervals. One large, fierce kudana was stuffed and stood on its hind legs at the entrance to the hall, sharp teeth bared. Qui-Gon reflected that it was one of the least appetizing dining halls he'd ever been in.

   The odor of roasting meat filled their nostrils as they followed King Frane to the main table set up near the pit. Smoke blew in their faces. Obi-Wan coughed, then stared in distaste at the bloody carcass revolving over the flame. Qui-

Gon was sure his usually ravenous young Padawan would not have much of an appetite this evening.

"Sit down, sit down," King Frane urged them as he took a seat at the head of the long table. "No, Taroon. Let the Jedi sit next to me."

A tall, light-blue Rutanian with coiled braids arranged in loops around his head stepped back and glowered at the Jedi.

"My son, Prince Taroon," King Frane said. Qui-Gon turned to greet him, but King Frane waved his hand, and Taroon took a place at the other side of his father. "Let's talk about Leed. That's the reason you're here, eh?"

Qui-Gon sat as a server placed a heaping plate of meat in front of him. He nodded his thanks.

"Prince Leed has decided to stay on Senali —" he began.

"Decided!" King Frane interrupted with a roar. He pounded the table. "So that lying dinko Meenon tells me! My son has been kidnapped!"

"But you yourself saw the holocom," Qui-Gon pointed out. "I have seen it, too. Prince Leed seems sincere."

"He has been coerced, or threatened," King Frane insisted, forking up a huge piece of meat. He shook his fork at Qui-Gon. "Or they gave him one of their potions. They are primitives. They can use herbs and plants to cloud the mind. Leed would never decide to stay. Never!"

Suddenly, even as he stared fiercely at Qui-Gon, Frane's large green eyes filled with tears. He picked up his napkin and began to mop his streaming eyes. "My oldest child. My treasure. Why won't he face me?" He blew his nose in his napkin and brooded. When he next looked at the Jedi, his face wore a mask of anger. "It is the dirty Senalis who made him do this!" he bellowed. "Why will he not come and face me?"

Perhaps because he is afraid of you, Qui-Gon thought. But he could not say it aloud. The king's changes of mood were startling, but they seemed sincere.

"What am I to do, Jedi?" King Frane forked the meat again and chewed vigorously. "Declare war?"

"Naturally we oppose such a step," Qui-Gon said. "That's why we are here. We can meet with Leed and assess the situation."

"Bring him home," King Frane said. "And eat your dinner. It is the best Rutan has to offer."

Qui-Gon took polite bites. "Meenon has agreed to our coming."

"He is a pig! He is a savage!" King Frane cried. "Do not believe a word he says. He stole my son. What does he know of loyalty? My son is a jewel. I kept up with his progress on their filthy planet. They have annual contests of speed and endurance and skill. He has won every year since he was thirteen. He is a jewel, I tell you. A natural leader!" He thumped the table. "Meant to be my heir. He is the only one who can succeed me! Everything I have, everyone around me is worthless if I cannot have my firstborn son follow me."

Qui-Gon glanced at Taroon. The younger son was pretending not to listen, but King Frane's bellow was certainly audible to him. Why did his father treat him as though he were invisible? He was only a year younger than Leed, a thin, awkward young man with long arms and legs. Was he worthless to his father?

"I will read the truth in Leed's eyes," King Frane continued, heaping another helping of meat onto Qui-Gon's still full plate. "Bring him to me, and I will know. If they will not let him go, I will invade their planet and bring them to their knees. You tell Meenon that."

"Jedi will not deliver a threat," Qui-Gon said firmly. "We will try to persuade your son to come back. We will not force him, or force the government of Senali. But if we bring him back, you cannot force him to stay. I must have your word on that."

"Yes, yes, you have my word. But Leed will

want to stay, I guarantee you. The boy knows his duty. I will send my younger son Taroon with you to deliver the threat to Meenon. He will also take Leed's place on Senali when my boy returns home."

"I will not allow Taroon to deliver a threat, either," Qui-Gon said. "If that is your objective, Taroon must stay behind. His presence could compromise a diplomatic mission. Meenon could feel pressured by the presence of someone from the royal family. Besides, Jedi always negotiate alone."

King Frane tore off a piece of meat with his sharp yellow teeth. Craftiness gleamed in his eyes. "I have just signed an order to imprison Meenon's daughter, Yaana, here on Rutan. I hear she is just as beloved to Meenon as Leed is to me. Let him know the pain of a grieving father! What do you think of that, Jedi?"

"It is a mistake," Qui-Gon said quietly. "Meenon will take it as a provocation. It will bring you close to war. I don't think you want that, no matter what you say. Your people do not want war."

"My people want what I tell them to want!" King Frane bellowed furiously. "Am I not king?"

Qui-Gon didn't blink. "We will allow Taroon to accompany us if you rescind your order to imprison Yaana."

King Frane stopped chewing and gave Qui-Gon a hard stare that lasted several moments. Then he slammed his hand down on the table again. "Done! The Jedi is clever!" He turned to the rest of the table, beaming. "The Jedi will bring Leed home again!"

The rest of the royal party erupted in cheers.

King Frane turned back to Qui-Gon. "In three days," he said. "That is all I give you. If you don't return with Leed, Yaana gets thrown into the foulest prison on Rutan." In another abrupt change of mood, he slapped Qui-Gon on the back. "Now enjoy!"

The rest of the royal party now felt free to relish their food. Conversation rose and buzzed amongst them.

Obi-Wan leaned over and spoke to Qui-Gon. "Taroon does not seem happy to be accompanying us," he said in a low tone.

"I noticed that," Qui-Gon answered. "Yet the negotiation went well. I wanted Taroon with us all along. I suspected that King Frane would imprison Yaana. We have bought her a few more days of freedom."

"But how did you know these things?" Obi-Wan asked, puzzled.

"Find the emotion, predict the deed," Qui-Gon replied. "It was a natural step — it is the only thing King Frane has to threaten Meenon with. King Frane is the type of ruler to lash out in the only way he can. Yet he is afraid of war, so he will allow himself to be persuaded to wait. Now all we have to do is bring back Leed. If we believe he is sincere and wants to remain on Senali, we must help him reconcile his father to his decision. If nothing goes wrong and every party acts with honesty and forgiveness, the situation will resolve itself."

Qui-Gon glanced over at Taroon. The young Rutanian had not joined in the feasting or conversation, but had kept his arms folded. His eyes were watchful and sullen.

"So you don't see danger ahead?" Obi-Wan asked.

Qui-Gon gave a brief smile. "I see tangled loyalties and the potential for misunderstandings. And even the smallest misunderstandings can bring danger when a situation is as volatile as this one. Words do not always echo what is in the heart. And things are rarely as simple as they appear."

CHAPTER 4

From above, the planet Senali looked like a shining blue jewel. So much of its surface was water that it reflected light and seemed to shimmer. As their transport skimmed over the surface toward Meenon's landing platform, Obi-Wan thought he had never seen such a beautiful world.

The seas seemed to hold a thousand shades of blue and green. Chains of islands dotted the water like necklaces. Lush green foliage and blooming flowers dotted the islands and were planted on the docks of the floating cities. Many of the structures were fashioned out of the branches and fronds of a native tree with bright red bark.

They landed on the royal landing platform and were greeted by several members of the chief's guard. Senali were the same species as Rutanians, but they had a silvery cast to their skin due to the tiny scales that covered their bodies. They were excellent swimmers with unusually strong breath control. Unlike Rutanians, their hair was worn short, and many of them wore headpieces and necklaces fashioned from coral and shells.

The Jedi and Taroon followed the guards into Meenon's dwelling. It was a long, low building that floated on the waters of a deep, green lagoon. The guards led them to an interior courtyard that had been transformed into a blooming garden, with drooping fronds that shaded them from the hot sun.

Meenon was tending to the garden, but straightened up and gave a formal bow to the Jedi when they arrived. He was dressed in a linen tunic and was barefoot. A simple headdress of white shells circled his shaved head.

"I am honored to have the Jedi on my beautiful planet," he said.

"We are honored to be here," Qui-Gon responded. He introduced himself, Obi-Wan, and Taroon. "We would like to see Prince Leed as soon as possible."

"Ah." Meenon looked down at the basket of flowers in his hand. He touched one bloom. "We have a small problem."

Beside him, Obi-Wan felt Taroon tense.

"Problem?" Qui-Gon asked neutrally.

Meenon looked up. "Leed has gone into hiding."

Qui-Gon did not react, but studied the leader carefully.

Taroon threw his chest out in a challenge. "What a surprise to hear my brother has disappeared! And you should refer to my brother by his title. He is *Prince* Leed. You show him disrespect."

Meenon bristled. "We do not believe in titles on Senali. Titles make divisions. We are all equal on Senali, unlike on your barbaric world."

Taroon's eyes glinted. "Unlike primitives, we value our bloodlines."

Qui-Gon inserted himself smoothly into the conversation before it could flare into open argument. "You say that Leed has disappeared. He left no word of where he was going?"

"No," Meenon said, turning his back to Taroon. "I do not know where he is."

Taroon put himself in front of Meenon again. "And you'll swear to this?" he demanded, eyes flashing.

Meenon gazed at Taroon. "I do not need to swear. I do not lie."

Qui-Gon spoke a beat more quickly than his usual reserve. Obi-Wan knew that he was trying to restrain Taroon without seeming to. "This is unfortunate."

Meenon shrugged. "He knew of your coming. I assume that is why he is in hiding. He does not want to return to Rutan."

"We are not here to force him," Qui-Gon said. "We only wish to talk to him."

"I assured him that if he met with you I would not allow him to be taken back to Rutan by force," Meenon said. "Apparently he has taken matters into his own hands despite my advice."

"We will search for him, with your permission," Qui-Gon said as Taroon fumed beside him. "Can we question the family who brought him up?"

"Here on Senali we live in clans," Meenon said. "I entrusted him to my sister's clan, the Banoosh-Walores. They live one kilometer to the west, on Clear Lake. You are welcome to question them."

Qui-Gon nodded. "We will be in touch."

"I wish you ease and serenity," Meenon said, bowing.

Obi-Wan could feel Taroon's anger as they walked out of the courtyard to exit Meenon's dwelling.

"He wishes us ease and serenity after such news?" Taroon said, disgusted. "He was mocking us!"

"It is a traditional good-bye of the Senali," Qui-Gon remarked mildly.

"This is intolerable!" Taroon continued. "He plays us for fools!"

"Your father will not take this news well," Qui-Gon said. "He will be angry, as you are."

"I am nothing like my father," Taroon said through his teeth.

"I wonder if Meenon knows more than he is telling," Obi-Wan wondered.

"Of course he does," Taroon spit out. "All Senali are treacherous. This is simply a tactic to delay us."

"Let's hope we can learn something from his sister's clan," Qui-Gon said. "Until then, let us remain calm."

They walked out into the bright sunlight. Suddenly Taroon wheeled and kicked a tall flowering bush that stood near the entrance to the dwelling. He attacked it in a frenzy, fists flailing and feet flying. Red petals showered from the bush and soon were strewn all over the walkway.

"Well, I see you have inherited your father's temper, at least," Qui-Gon remarked.

CHAPTER 5

The red-and-blue dwelling of the Banoosh-Walore clan was part of the main city of Senali, which was built on floating docks and platforms. The various islands were connected to each other by graceful silver bridges that arched over the blue water.

The brightly painted structure sprawled over a large area. The main part of the dwelling was merely a frame connected with walls of woven fronds that rolled up to let in sea breezes. One wall was let down to protect those inside from the sun. The rest of the house was open on three sides. There was no need to knock. They could see the members of the clan gathered in the large central room.

A tall female Senali with pink coral studded in her short dark hair beckoned them inside. "Meenon said you were arriving. Welcome, welcome! Let me introduce you. I am Ganeed,

Meenon's sister. These are my sons Hinen and Jaret, and this is Jaret's wife Mesan and their daughter Tawn. That is Drenna, my youngest, and Wek, my sister's boy, and Nonce, and my husband, Garth, and my father, Tonai. Oh, and there's my elder mother, Nin, and the baby, we call her Bu."

A small boy tugged on Ganeed's tunic. "And me!"

She put a hand on his head. "Of course, Tinta. I didn't forget you. I saved you for last because you are so important."

Obi-Wan nodded to the bustling, busy group. He knew he would never be able to keep the names straight. He had recently begun memory training at the Temple. He could redraw a tech blueprint that he had only glimpsed for ten seconds or recite a complicated formula he had just heard once, but he still was not very skilled at remembering the names of a crowd of living beings. He counted on Qui-Gon to do that.

One of Ganeed's sons, either Jaret or Hinen, sat at a long table, peeling fruit with a young Senali female. Was it Wek or Mesan? The elder Senali stood at a stove, stirring something in a pot that smelled delicious. A young man rocked the baby, and a slender young Senali female with silvery hair sat in a corner, mending a fishing net. Everyone seemed to be talking at once, and he could not distinguish any one voice except for Ganeed, who called for everyone to be quiet. Finally she picked up a pot and spoon and banged on the pot bottom. The clan members finally were still.

"There," she said with satisfaction.

Taroon remained a stiff presence by Obi-Wan's side. Obi-Wan felt just as awkward. He admired the way Qui-Gon swung his leg over a stool and began to speak earnestly with Tinta, admiring a toy in the small boy's hand. Obi-Wan did not have the knack of ease with strangers.

"I should say right away that we have no idea where Leed is," Ganeed said, without waiting for Qui-Gon to ask a question. "He left a note which said only that it would be better for his clan if we did not know."

Qui-Gon nodded. "I see."

One of Ganeed's sons spoke up. "That is just like Leed. He does not like to cause trouble."

His wife nodded. "He is very kind."

Ganeed's husband, Garth, chimed in. "Even as a boy his kindness endeared him to everyone. It is a pity such trouble has come to him."

"A pity his father will not listen to reason," Hinen — or was it Jaret? — said.

Obi-Wan saw Taroon's hands clench into

fists, hidden by his tunic. The prince was struggling to contain himself. Qui-Gon had warned him to let the Jedi do all the talking.

The elder Nin looked up from the stove. "He always had his own way of doing things, our Leed. Set the table for the meal, Wek, if you please. Will our guests join us?"

"I'm afraid we cannot, but I thank you," Qui-Gon said politely.

The boy Wek began to set places at the long table. He appeared only a year or two younger than Leed. Were they close companions? Obi-Wan wondered.

The same thought must have crossed Qui-Gon's mind. "Is there any special place Leed is fond of going, Wek?" he asked in a kind tone.

Wek placed a bowl on the table. "Well, he likes to swim," he said.

"When he isn't sailing," Jaret or Hinen said.

"True, Jaret," the other son said. At least Obi-Wan could now keep the two of them straight.

"I love to sail!" Tinta cried. "Leed taught me how, and —"

"But he was always walking in the forest, don't forget," Mesan interrupted, turning to Jaret. "That's where I would look —" She stopped abruptly to pick up the baby, Bu, who had begun to fuss.

"He only goes in spring," Nonce broke in over the wailing of the baby. He walked to the stove and began to help Nin, slicing bread for the meal. "He —"

"He goes in summer, too! Everyone goes in summer!" Wek argued. "You just don't notice because —"

"Who goes in summer? It's too hot," Tawn broke in. "Leed likes the cool water and long swims. And —"

"Food," Hinen said, leaning over to snatch a piece of bread off the counter. "Leed likes his meals. He'll be back before long — ow!" he cried as Nonce rapped his knuckles with a wooden spoon.

The baby began to cry again, and Jaret took her from Mesan's arms. Tinta began to quarrel with the other young boy.

"I agree with Jaret," Tonai said serenely over the noise of the baby crying and the voices raised in a quarrel. "I would search the forest, not the sea."

"I said the sea, not the forest!" Jaret protested. "You never listen to a word —"

"What do I know anyway?" Tonai broke in, shrugging.

"You know plenty, old man," the elder Nin said. "Except when to go to bed."

"I know when to eat," Tonai said, seating himself at the table with great pleasure. Nin ladled some soup in a bowl.

"I think he went back to Rutan on his own," Garth said. "That would make sense. He did not want to worry us."

A storm of argument broke out over this last suggestion. Jaret and Hinen began to shout. Tinta upset the plate full of bread. Bu began to hiccup, and Jaret handed her to Ganeed.

Ganeed smiled at the Jedi over the baby's shoulder as she patted her back. "You see? We have no idea where Leed could be."

"Even Drenna doesn't know," Tinta said.

Qui-Gon cast his keen gaze on the young boy. "Is Drenna a special friend of Leed's, Tinta?"

"She is closest to him in age," Ganeed said, handing the baby to Mesan.

Obi-Wan shot a searching glance at Drenna for the first time. Her close-cropped hair almost matched the silvery cast to her dark-blue skin. She raised her silver eyes to the Jedi.

"You can see this place is confusing," she said, making a wry face. "Maybe Leed just wanted some peace and quiet to make up his mind. I think he will return soon."

"Drenna, help Wek set the table," Nin called. "Go sit down, boy, you are underfoot."

"Let's eat," Jaret said. "I'm hungry."

"Well, come to the table, then," Nin scolded. "I can't do everything for you."

Drenna sprang up and began to ladle the food into bowls.

"Yes, perhaps Leed will return soon," Qui-Gon said. "He will miss his clan. As you miss him."

Ganeed's eyes suddenly filled with tears. "As we do," she said softly.

A silence fell over the clan for the first time. Obi-Wan could read sorrow on each face. Leed was truly loved, he saw.

For a moment, all they heard were Bu's tiny hiccups as she nestled her downy head against her mother's shoulder.

"This is a waste of time," Taroon suddenly said. "They won't tell us anything."

"We should leave you to your midday meal," Qui-Gon said graciously, bowing to the clan.

"We wish you ease and serenity," Ganeed said, smiling through tear-filled eyes. "And if you find Leed, please protect him."

"We shall," Qui-Gon promised.

They retreated down the walkway that joined the structure to the main dock, then started back toward Meenon's dwelling.

"They were no help at all," Taroon complained.

"I don't know how Leed could stand to live with so many people."

"They seem to enjoy one another's company," Qui-Gon observed.

"They certainly like to talk," Obi-Wan added. He had felt awkward among the clan, but he had also felt their warmth and their obvious affection for one another.

"Yet they did not say a thing," Qui-Gon said. "Did you notice that, Padawan?"

Obi-Wan thought about it. "They all contradicted each other's guesses. It seemed as though they were giving us leads, but they weren't."

"Exactly. And then when we turned our attention to Drenna, suddenly everyone needed to eat. Come this way." Qui-Gon headed down a smaller floating dock that was perpendicular to the main passageway. A small floating garden was set up for the benefit of the dwellers of the floating city. Qui-Gon paused behind a lush bush studded with orange blooms.

"What are we doing?" Taroon asked irritably. "We have no time to pick flowers."

Qui-Gon didn't answer. Obi-Wan saw that from here they had a perfect view of the front of the clan's dwelling. In another moment, Drenna came outside. She stood on the dock and looked to her right, then her left. She had buckled a supply belt around her tunic, and Obi-Wan could see its pouch was full.

She turned and quickly walked down the dock in the opposite direction.

"Let's go," Qui-Gon said.

"Why should we follow a Senali on her useless errands?" Taroon scowled.

"Because she will bring us to Leed," Qui-Gon answered.

CHAPTER 6

At first it was easy to follow Drenna. Senalis strolled along the docks on this fine day, pausing to purchase flowers and food at various markets that were set up along the way. The Jedi and Taroon could melt into the crowd and keep her in sight.

The Jedi had already adapted to the idea that the ground was not firm under their feet. The docks swayed and bobbed in the gentle roll of the sea. Taroon had more trouble. Occasionally he would stumble and his skin would flush to a bluish rose.

"What kind of a world builds its cities on water?" he grumbled after he had stumbled again and narrowly escaped tumbling off the dock. "I don't see how my brother can stand this awful place."

Qui-Gon lifted an eyebrow at Obi-Wan in a private gesture. Obi-Wan smiled. He knew what his Master was thinking. Senali had turquoise seas, blooming gardens, and, from the looks of it, a peaceful and content population. Taroon harbored the prejudice of Rutanians, most of whom had not set foot on Senali since the war that had divided them forever. They considered Senalis lazy primitives who had not built a thriving culture or economy and who lived only for pleasure.

The floating city stretched over several kilometers. Drenna led them over bridges and walkways into different sections, some with brightly painted multistoried buildings, some with eccentric structures that bobbed cheerfully on the water. They passed rows and rows of docks with different crafts tied to the pilings. The crowd began to thin, and they hung back, keeping Drenna just in sight.

At last Drenna turned toward one of the silver bridges that connected the floating city to the mainland. She hurried over the bridge and disappeared down a road that curved around a dense thicket of trees. They quickly followed.

Trees lined the road that verged the shore. The branches were heavy with green fronds that bent the limbs down to the ground, their feathery leaves lying like lace on the sandy road. Deep green shadows flickered, and every now and then a glimpse of the turquoise sea appeared like a startling vision through the thick curtain of leaves.

Qui-Gon tapped into the Force to help him track Drenna. He had to be alert to the smallest sounds ahead, to the disturbance in the air he could feel as she passed through it.

Senali was a small world, and most of the population traveled by sea or on foot. The Jedi did not see many speeders or other craft that moved through air. Small transports occasionally buzzed by, carrying goods and food.

The road split into two main roads and a narrower trail that wound through the trees. Drenna was no longer in sight. Qui-Gon hesitated only a moment before determining that she had taken the narrow trail.

Obi-Wan kept close on his heels. The path slowly narrowed until they had to go single file. The firmly packed soil of the road had changed to a loose, powdery sand that sucked at their footsteps. Again, Taroon had trouble keeping up.

"There's more sand in my boots than on the ground," he muttered. "Why don't these people build decent roads?"

Qui-Gon held up a hand and they stopped. He closed his eyes, listening intently.

"She is running now," he said, surprised. "We must go faster."

They quickened their pace. Taroon stopped

complaining and concentrated on keeping up with them. The sound of the surf covered the noise of their feet slapping against the sand.

They turned a corner and saw that the trail ran straight into the high wall of a sheer cliff. There was still room to walk around it, along a narrow strip of beach. A wave lapped at their heels as they skirted the cliff wall, avoiding the rocks that were studded with sharp coral that could slice into skin.

They found themselves in a beautiful cove with a beach that curved like a quarter moon. Sheer cliffs surrounded them.

The beach was empty except for a slight figure in the distance. Qui-Gon had been right: Drenna was running now, jogging easily down the beach toward the end of the far curve.

"Does she realize now that she's being followed?" Obi-Wan asked as they picked up their pace. They kept in the shadow of the cliff in case she turned around.

Suddenly, Qui-Gon stopped short. He looked up at the cliff, then back at the churning sea.

"She always knew she was being followed," he said. "We must go back."

Taroon looked behind them. "Look at that. The path is already cut off."

Waves now thundered against the cliff wall. If they tried to return, they would be trapped. The tide was strong enough to batter them against the sharp rocks.

Water suddenly foamed around their ankles.

"The tide is coming in," Obi-Wan said.

"The tides are famous on Senali," Qui-Gon said, his eyes now moving over the cliff face. "The four moons make them swift and extreme."

Drenna had disappeared around the cliff face at the far end of the beach. Obi-Wan calculated the distance, then stepped back as a wave of alarming force hit him at the knees.

They would not make it, he realized.

Taroon came to the same conclusion as he glanced at the faces of the Jedi.

"She led us into a trap!" he cried.

CHAPTER 7

Qui-Gon was already calculating their next move. "We can run to the end of the cove that way. The tide will catch up with us, so we'll have to swim around the cliff. At least there are no rocks on that end. We can make it."

"But I can't swim!" Taroon cried. "No Rutanian can. Swimming is for primitives."

"Right now, swimming is for survival," Qui-Gon said dryly. He scanned the sea. He saw roiling eddies and a tidal pattern that was extremely treacherous. He and Obi-Wan could make it — they were Jedi. But he could not risk Taroon's life. He would not want to endanger Obi-Wan, either.

They quickly backed up as the next wave hit them waist-high. The strength of it was astonishing. Taroon almost fell, and Qui-Gon caught him by the arm and steadied him.

"I hate the sea," Taroon muttered. He wiped his wet hair out of his eyes.

"How do you feel about climbing?" Qui-Gon asked.

Taroon eyed the cliff. "You've got to be kidding!" he exclaimed. "There's no way to climb that cliff."

Qui-Gon did not answer. He knew there was no time to waste. He slipped his electrobinoculars from his utility belt and scanned the cliff, looking for handholds and footholds. There weren't many. And the cliff was so high that their liquid cable launchers wouldn't reach the top. There was nothing to hook them around on the cliff face, either.

The water foamed around his knees and tried to suck him backward. Taroon clutched Obi-Wan for support.

"How could you have gotten us into this?" he asked the Jedi. "That female has made fools of us!"

Qui-Gon focused the electrobinoculars. He saw a tiny fissure in the rock, just enough for the spike tip of his liquid cable launcher to find purchase. It would have to do.

He replaced the electrobinoculars and withdrew the launcher, motioning for Obi-Wan to do the same.

"Wait until mine hooks, then launch yours," he directed.

Qui-Gon got it in one try, which was fortunate, for the next wave was up to the Jedi's shoulders. Obi-Wan got his launcher anchored on the second try, at the next ebb. They tested the line, and it held.

"Go," Qui-Gon said tersely. He motioned to Taroon to take hold of the cable. He would stay behind the prince in order to protect him from falling.

He only hoped the launchers would raise them high enough to escape the tide. The form of vegetation clinging to the wall told him that most of the cliff went underwater at high tide. Qui-Gon did not look forward to hanging in midair and watching the sea rise ever closer to them.

He watched as his Padawan zoomed ahead, pulled by the cable. He dangled above their heads.

"Hold on," Qui-Gon instructed Taroon. The cable retracted, bringing them high above the beach. They hung suspended near the cliff face.

"Do you think the water will reach us?" Taroon asked, beginning to turn around.

"Don't look down," Qui-Gon said sharply, but it was too late. Taroon had seen how high they were. He flinched, and his knee banged against the cliff. He let out a hoarse cry and closed his eyes.

"I am right behind you, Taroon," Qui-Gon told him. "We can get through this if you don't panic. The cable is holding our weight. Don't look down."

Taroon took a deep breath. "I'll be all right," he said. "I was just surprised, that's all."

Qui-Gon admired his composure. He knew Taroon was afraid.

"See if you can find a foothold," Qui-Gon directed. "That will take the weight off your arms. You can't fall. You're fastened to the cable."

Qui-Gon searched the cliff area overhead. He could not see another fissure. They would have to hang here and hope the sea wouldn't rise to drown them. He knew that he and Obi-Wan could hang here for hours if they had to. But he was not sure about Taroon.

"The tide is still rising," Obi-Wan said to him quietly. "The waves could break over our heads. Maybe we should put on our breathers."

Qui-Gon nodded. It was a good suggestion. "In a minute." He did not want to panic Taroon until he had to.

"Can't we go higher?" Taroon asked nervously. "I can feel the spray of the waves."

"We are all right for now," Qui-Gon said. But

he could see that within moments the crashing waves could hit them.

Suddenly, he saw another cable shoot down from the overhang a hundred meters up. It dangled between Qui-Gon and Obi-Wan.

"Take it!" someone shouted. "It will hold all of you! The sea is rising!"

Qui-Gon reached out and tested it. He exchanged a glance with Obi-Wan.

Should we do it? Obi-Wan asked silently.

We have no choice, Qui-Gon answered him.

Obi-Wan nodded. He grasped the cable first. Taroon came next. Then Qui-Gon. The three of them now hung on a cable and had to trust whoever was overhead.

The cable retracted slowly, bringing them smoothly up the face of the cliff toward the top. Obi-Wan clambered over, then Taroon. Qui-Gon was last to tumble over the edge. He shot to his feet immediately.

A tall, sturdy local stood before them. A necklace of pink coral was hung around his neck and circled his wrist. He grinned at them.

"Glad you could make it."

Taroon gasped. "Leed!"

CHAPTER 8

Leed joyfully rushed toward his brother. They threw their arms around each other.

"My brother!" Leed cried.

"My brother!" Taroon answered.

"How it pleases me to have your company," Leed said. "You've grown almost as tall as I am."

"Taller," Taroon said with a smile.

They stepped back. Leed turned to the Jedi.

"And you must be the Jedi, sent to bring me back to Rutan."

"I am Qui-Gon Jinn and this is Obi-Wan Kenobi," Qui-Gon said. "We are here to ensure that you are not being forced to remain or manipulated."

"You can see I am neither," Leed said.

"I have not had time to see much of anything yet," Qui-Gon responded in a friendly way.

Leed turned to his brother. "I must apologize

for Drenna. She wasn't trying to kill you, just to protect me."

"She may not have meant to, but she almost *did* kill me," Taroon said darkly. "I could have drowned!"

"Yet you did not," Leed said. "Come out, Drenna. You see they will not harm me."

Leaves rustled, and Drenna emerged from the blue-green shadows of the overgrown trees. She had blended into the shades and shadows perfectly. Taroon was surprised to see her, but Obi-Wan saw from Qui-Gon's expression that he had sensed her presence.

Drenna stood apart from the group. She eyed them warily, clearly not convinced they had not come to abduct Leed.

She turned to the Jedi and Taroon. "Well? You see that Leed is here of his own free will. Now you can return to Rutan."

Qui-Gon turned to Leed. "If you truly wish to remain on Senali, you should face your father with your decision."

Leed shook his head firmly. "Nothing can make me return. He will force me to stay, imprison me."

"If we give you our word that we will not allow your father to force you to stay, will you come?" Qui-Gon asked.

"It is not that I do not respect the great powers of the Jedi," Leed said slowly. "I do not wish to offend you. But my father has wiles and treacheries you have not seen. There are things you can't protect me from."

"That is not true!" Taroon protested.

"If you feel as you do, we have a problem," Qui-Gon said to Leed, his tone pleasant but firm. "You will not return to Rutan. And we will find it hard to leave Senali without you."

Leed met Qui-Gon's gaze stonily. Neither of them moved. Obi-Wan's eyes went from one to the other. In both of them, he saw conviction that would not be swayed. Qui-Gon was such a strong presence that it was hard to imagine going up against his will.

Yet he had done the same once.

On Melida/Daan, he had met Qui-Gon's resolute will with his own. They had clashed and been torn apart as a result. Obi-Wan had believed then with all his heart that he was right. He had come to see that he had been blinded by loyalty to a cause not his own.

But what about Leed? He had lived on Senali for most of his childhood. He had come to manhood here. Obi-Wan could not help feeling sympathetic to Leed's wishes. It was obvious that he loved his brother. But it was clear that his bond with his adopted sister, Drenna, was just as strong.

In an abrupt change of mood that reminded Obi-Wan of Leed's father, Leed broke the tension with a shrug and a warm smile. "Well, then. If you are to be my guests, I shall have to bring you to my home. Come."

Leed led them through a maze of overgrown paths and then struck out through a marsh, moving easily from only slightly submerged rocks to firm ground undetectable to most eyes. The air here was thick and close. Brightly colored flying creatures buzzed and sang overhead.

At last they emerged high above the shoreline on a cliff similar to the one they had left. But here the sea was gentle as the land curved, making a natural harbor. A chain of islands were in the distance.

They hiked down to the beach where Leed and Drenna tossed aside huge fronds to uncover a boat.

They glided over the calm, aquamarine sea, hugging the shore until they came to a lagoon surrounded by a cluster of small islands. A hut fashioned of tree trunks and woven grasses sat on a floating dock offshore. Leed tied the craft to the side and they disembarked.

"The Nali-Erun clan lives on the far island,"

Leed said, pointing to a lush green island a few kilometers away. "They watch out for me."

"All Senali watch out for one another," Drenna said.

"Why are you hiding in such a remote area, Leed?" Qui-Gon asked. "Are you afraid your father's reach could extend this far?"

Leed nodded as he crouched to untangle some fishing line. "I spoke to my father so many times. We were in regular communication, the way I was with Taroon. But after I told him of my decision, he cut me off. He refused to hear me. He said Meenon had influenced me. If it pains him to hear the deepest wish of my heart, why should I go on trying to speak with him?"

Qui-Gon sat down on the dock next to Leed so that they could be at eye level. He began to help untangle the line. "Because he is your father," he said. "And he is afraid he has lost his son."

Leed's hands went still. "I am still his son," he said firmly. "And if he would not be so stubborn, we could be in constant contact. I could come to Rutan for visits, and he could come here. But ever since the war, there is no travel between the two worlds. I would like to change that."

Qui-Gon nodded. "That would be a good change. That is one of the things you could do as ruler of Rutan. You would have it in your power to change many things. Why don't you want to help your world, your people?"

Leed gazed out over the lagoon. "Because Rutan does not feel like my world. Its people don't feel like my people. It is hard to explain. But I found myself here. Underneath this sun I feel at home. And if Rutan is no longer my home I do not have the right to rule it. Senali is in my blood and bones. It is something I cannot help. Even as a small boy, I did not feel part of Rutan. I was afraid to leave my family and come here. But as soon as I stepped off the transport, I felt at home." He glanced at Drenna. "I have found myself here," he said.

Obi-Wan saw hurt on Taroon's face as Leed spoke. As his brother shared a private smile with Drenna, Taroon's face tightened with anger.

Jedi were supposed to remain impartial. But Obi-Wan felt Leed's words strike his heart. Now instead of connecting them to what he'd felt on Melida/Daan, he connected them to the Temple. It was not where he was born. The Jedi Masters were not his parents. Yet it was home. He knew that in his heart and bones. He believed that Leed felt the same.

"I understand all that you say," Qui-Gon said.

"And I ask you this: Is your decision to act according to your heart worth plunging two worlds into war? Are your individual desires so important?"

Leed angrily tossed aside the line. "I do not start a war. My father does."

"He does it for you," Qui-Gon told him.

"He does it for himself!" Leed protested.

Taroon had been restraining himself, but now he stepped forward. "I don't understand you, brother," he said. "What is it that is worth so much to you? A world of strangers? How can you risk the peace of your home planet just for your own desires?"

"You don't understand," Leed said, shaking his head.

"No, I do not!" Taroon shouted angrily. "I do not understand this deep wish of your heart. Is it more important for you to live with primitives than to take up your birthright?"

"Primitives?" Drenna exclaimed. "How dare you call us that!"

Taroon turned on her. "Where are your great cities?" he demanded. "A cluster of shacks bobbing on the sea. Where is your culture, your art, your trade, your wealth? On Rutan, we have centers of learning. We develop new medicines and technologies. We explore the galaxy —"

"Our wealth is in our land and our seas and

our people," Drenna said, facing him down. "Our culture and our art is part of our daily lives. You have been on Senali for half a day. How dare you judge us?"

"I know your world," Taroon said. "Any culture you have the Rutanians brought to you."

"I know you brought your taste for blood sports and your arrogance," Drenna shot back. "We got rid of all that when we got rid of you. If we kill a creature, we kill it for food. We do not kill it for sport, or to sell its skin. And you call us primitives!"

"I do not think it helpful to debate the differences between Rutan and Senali when —" Qui-Gon began, but Drenna interrupted him furiously.

"Only a fool debates with ignorance," she said fiercely. "I do not debate! I speak truth."

"You speak with your own arrogance," Taroon exclaimed. "You don't know Rutan any better than I know Senali! All you know is prejudice and disdain."

"You came here to look down on us," Drenna said with contempt. "I saw that at once. Why do you think your brother should listen to your opinion when it is full of your own bias?"

"Because I am his family!" Taroon roared.

"As am I!" Drenna countered.

"You are not his family," Taroon shouted. "You were just his caretakers. We are his blood!"

"No, Taroon." Leed stepped between them. "Drenna is my sister as you are my brother. And she is right. This is what I leave behind on Rutan," he continued, his voice rising to match Drenna's and Taroon's. "This attitude that you are superior to the Senalis. You do not know Senali, nor do you wish to. Do you really want to live the life of our father, living only to chase animals and feast until you cannot move? Do you want your life goal to be the gathering of more and more wealth, just for the purpose of possessing it?"

"Is that what you think of us?" Taroon demanded. "Now I *know* you've been brainwashed! There is more to Rutan than that, and more to our father as well."

"I spoke hastily," Leed said, gathering control of his voice. "I apologize. Yes, there are good things on Rutan. But they are not things that interest me."

Taroon grasped his brother's arms. "Leed, how could you want to live like this?"

Leed shook him off with an angry gesture.

Drenna turned to Leed. "You see? I told you of the contempt the Rutanians hold us in. Even your brother. You did not believe me. Now you must see that you can't go back."

"No," Leed said. "I can't go back."

"You cannot face our father because you know you are wrong," Taroon said. "You are afraid of him."

"I am not afraid of him," Leed countered angrily. "I do not trust him. There is a difference. I don't want to be under his influence. I am *glad* I was brought up by others, without being exposed to all his faults. You know after our mother died that there was no one to check him. He is not a bad man, Taroon. Just a bad father."

Taroon's face was tight. "And I was brought up by his side, inheriting all his bad traits, while you have all the good. Is that right?"

Leed took a breath. "That is not what I'm saying." He rubbed his hands over his hair in frustration. "I am not going back, Taroon."

"That is fine," Taroon said, his icy rage now burning hot. "I realize now that I was wrong to try to persuade you. Because even if you were to change your mind, I would not stay here in your place."

Qui-Gon exchanged a helpless glance with Obi-Wan. They had come to Senali hoping that gentle persuasion would help the situation. Qui-Gon had thought that brother to brother, the obvious affection between Leed and Taroon would bring them to common ground.

Instead, the two brothers were farther apart than ever. And the two worlds were now closer to war.

CHAPTER 9

Night fell swiftly on Senali. The four moons rose and stars appeared. Leed silently rolled out bedding for them. He placed a simple meal before them. No one spoke. Qui-Gon thought it better to let the tensions cool. He had found through long experience that one thing was the same for all cultures on different worlds: Even the most extreme crises looked better in the morning.

He lay on his sleep mat next to Obi-Wan. "What do you think, Padawan?" he asked softly. "Is Leed right or wrong?"

"That is not for me to say," Obi-Wan responded after a short silence. "I am to remain neutral."

"But I am asking you what you think," Qui-Gon said. "You can have a feeling. It does not have to affect your behavior."

Obi-Wan hesitated again. "I think that personal happiness is less important than duty."

Qui-Gon frowned. His Padawan had evaded the question. He had not lied, but he had not told the truth, either. Yet Qui-Gon would not chide him. The evasion came from a place of goodness. Somehow Obi-Wan must feel that to tell Qui-Gon the truth would be wrong. Qui-Gon would let the question rest there. He would not push. He was learning how to be a Master as surely as Obi-Wan was learning how to be a Padawan.

Learn not to teach, you must, Yoda had told him. *As surely as you must guide, you must also be led.*

They fell asleep to the gentle slap of the waves against the dock. The sun rose, and they awoke to the sound of birds and the splash of fish in the sea.

"I'm afraid I have no more food," Leed said to them. His manner was friendlier than last night. Qui-Gon thought that was a good sign. It reinforced his decision not to push today. He would stand back and wait to see if Leed and Taroon could find each other.

Drenna had been awake for some time and had untangled fishing line and lined up short spears for each of them.

"On Senali, we are taught from an early age to be responsible for our own nourishment," she said to them. "If you wish to eat, you must fish."

"I am not hungry," Taroon said haughtily.

Drenna met his gaze steadily. "That is not true," she said. "You are hungry. And you are afraid."

Taroon bristled, and Qui-Gon gathered himself for another argument. He would not allow this one to go so far, he decided. A day of harmony would do them all good.

But before Taroon could speak, Drenna added in a gentler tone, "It is natural to fear water when you cannot swim. But I can teach you. Senali and Rutanians are the same species. If we can be expert swimmers, you can be, too."

Taroon hesitated.

"Of course," Drenna said, shrugging, "you might have a problem. You can't send seeker droids after fish. And if you hit them with a blaster, there goes your breakfast."

She smirked at Taroon. Drenna had thrown out a challenge, Qui-Gon saw.

"I can learn by myself," Taroon said.

"No, you can't. Do not worry," Drenna said in a soft tone. "I won't make fun of you. I had to learn myself, once."

Taroon rose stiffly and picked up some fishing line and a spear. "All right, then. Let's go."

With a whoop, Leed dove off the dock. Qui-Gon and Obi-Wan dove into the warm, clear water after him. Drenna took Taroon on the boat closer to shore to give him his first swimming lesson.

Qui-Gon and Obi-Wan donned their breathers as Leed treaded water.

"The principal source of food for many Senalis is the rocshore fish," he explained. "It has a spiny body with three large claws. If you take only one claw, the animal lives and grows another. You spear the fish through the tail, where it has no feeling. Then you grab the claw and twist it hard. Be careful or you can lose your fingers. You can watch me take a claw first, if you like."

"That sounds like a good idea," Qui-Gon said.

They dove deep into the lagoon, down where the water was cool and clear. Qui-Gon and Obi-Wan followed Leed as he easily speared one rocshore fish, then another, grasping a claw and twisting to sever it, then dropping it into the pouch he wore at his waist. Soon Obi-Wan and Qui-Gon had speared their own rocshores and their pouches were full of the meaty claws.

They were almost ready to return when they saw Taroon and Drenna swimming nearby. Taroon was gliding through the water. Drenna had been a good teacher. Taroon's long legs and arms coordinated with smooth strokes and powerful kicks. He did not seem awkward as he had on land. He speared one rocshore, then another. Drenna swam beside him, pointing out fish and spearing her own with deft, perfectly aimed shots.

When they surfaced, Taroon grinned, holding up his full pouch. Qui-Gon realized that he had never seen Taroon smile.

"Pretty good, for your first try," Drenna said. "You are a fast learner."

"You helped," he conceded.

"It took me weeks to learn how to swim that well," Leed told his brother admiringly.

Taroon turned his head to scan the shoreline. Qui-Gon saw that he was trying to conceal his pleasure at Leed's compliment. "Well, it's better than drowning," he said gruffly.

They swam toward the shore of the lagoon, where Leed and Drenna built a fire. They roasted the claws and cracked them open, squirting juice on the claw meat from tart fruit that Leed and Drenna had gathered.

It was a delicious meal. They ate their fill, then discovered that they still had more than half left over.

"We can take these to the Nali-Erun clan," he said.

They paddled over to the nearby island. The

clan had built their homes in the center of the island, underneath the cool shade of the trees. The structures were different from the ones in the main city. Here, they were built with leaves and reeds. They looked flimsy, and some looked ready to tumble down. When Leed held up his present of fish, children ran toward him hungrily.

"Why are they hungry?" Obi-Wan asked.

"They cannot fish in the lagoon," Leed explained in a low tone. "The Homd-Resa clan controls the surrounding seas. The two clans have recently been at odds. The Homd-Resa conducted a raid and destroyed much of their dwellings. The Nali-Erun had to rebuild quickly. They still have not recovered. And for months now they've had to live on fruit and what grains and fish they are able to trade for."

Taroon raised his thick eyebrows at Drenna. "All Senali watch out for each other?"

Drenna looked uncomfortable. "Naturally some clans have conflicts. I did not say Senali was a perfect world."

"Why doesn't Meenon step in?" Obi-Wan asked.

"Because the clans are self-governing," Drenna explained. "Meenon is more of a symbol to us than an actual leader."

The Nali-Erun clan happily distributed the fish

and offered the group some. Leed refused but took a bag of pashie, the sweet fruit that grew abundantly on the Nali-Eruns' trees.

Drenna also handed the head of the clan a pouch full of shells she had collected from the sea floor. The clan members held up each shell and admired it. One of the members began to string a few of the loveliest shells on a cord to fashion a necklace.

He held the finished necklace out to Drenna. She took it with a smile, then hesitated.

Her smile turned impish, and she turned to Taroon and placed it around his neck. "Now you are a real Senali," she said, tilting back her head and smiling up at him.

Taroon was startled. He touched the shells. His eyes met Leed's. "I am still Rutanian," he said. "But I am learning."

They caught small silver fish for the evening meal and Leed made a delicious stew. Taroon ladled it into bowls. Qui-Gon watched as the two brothers passed the bowls between them. There was an ease in their relationship now. The four moons rose, high and full, sending four silver paths down the dark water.

They sat underneath the wide dark sky. Qui-Gon stayed silent. He sensed something growing in Taroon, a new feeling the young man was struggling to voice. He hoped Taroon would find the courage to speak. Tomorrow was the third day. He would have to contact King Frane.

"I suppose we should be getting to sleep now," Leed said at last. "Thank you, Qui-Gon, for allowing us this day without trying to convince me to leave."

"It was a fine day," Taroon said hesitantly. "And I have come to a decision. I will not oppose your wish to stay here, brother. I see what draws you here. I spoke hastily this morning." He turned to the Jedi. "It is a fault I have. I'm sorry for my rudeness to you as well." He gave a wry grin. "You are right, Qui-Gon. I inherit my temper from my father."

"Thank you, brother," Leed said quietly. "You opened your mind and heart. I will do the same. I will return to Rutan and face our father."

"And I will take your place here until you return," Taroon said.

"Obi-Wan and I will ensure your safety," Qui-Gon promised Leed. "You will be free to return if you still wish to."

The brothers grasped each other's forearms in a show of affection.

"We will not let this divide us," Taroon said.

This was precisely what Qui-Gon had hoped for. Yet sadness hung in the air. Leed had taken the step to remove himself from his family.

Taroon had accepted his right to do this. It was clear that both brothers were heartbroken.

They all said good night. Obi-Wan rolled out his sleep mat next to Qui-Gon's. "Did you know that would happen?" he whispered. "Is that why you didn't challenge Leed today?"

"I hoped the day would bring reconciliation," Qui-Gon answered. "When Drenna offered to teach Taroon how to swim this morning, it was a good sign. I'm sure that Leed spoke to her about being kind to Taroon."

"But Leed was so angry last night," Obi-Wan said. "So was Drenna. Why would they turn around and be nice to Taroon?"

"Because he is Leed's brother," Qui-Gon answered. "Underneath everything, there is a bond between them. Drenna's loyalty is to Leed, so naturally she would help him if he asked."

"I don't understand," Obi-Wan said. "Everyone was so angry, and now everything is resolved. Can it really be so easy?"

"We are not back on Rutan yet. We shall see." Qui-Gon stretched out on the dock and gazed up at the sky. The mission was not over, he knew. He should not feel it was resolved yet. But he was pleased at how the brothers had handled their volatile feelings.

Unless it was too easy, as Obi-Wan had said.

Overhead, the sky curved above him, bright with silver moons and clusters of stars. Here on Senali the atmosphere turned the night sky a unique color, somewhere between navy and purple. It was at such times of hushed beauty that Qui-Gon felt the Force vibrate clearly, from the burning energy of the stars to the soft splash of a leaping fish.

"It is seldom that matters resolve themselves so easily," he said softly to Obi-Wan. "Let us hope it is so. Being a Jedi means we honor connections."

Obi-Wan nodded, yawning. It had been a long day. Slowly, his eyes closed. The gentle rocking of the structure soon lulled him to sleep. Qui-Gon felt himself beginning to slide into sleep as easily as he had slid into the warm lagoon.

He awoke with a start. He was instantly awake, alert for the next sound. He only heard silence, but he stood, his hand on his lightsaber.

Obi-Wan's eyes flew open. He jumped soundlessly to his feet. Something was wrong.

The tiniest sounds alerted him, the softest ripple of water. Qui-Gon dashed to the other side of the floating shelter.

A group of Senalis paddled a boat quickly

away, their skin smeared with white clay. A bound-and-gagged Leed sat slumped in the stern of the boat.

Qui-Gon searched for Leed's craft, which should have been tied to the dock. It did not surprise him to see it gone. They had most likely sunk it in the lagoon.

It was too far to swim and catch them.

Leed had been kidnapped right under their noses, just as Qui-Gon was no doubt dreaming of a benevolent galaxy of stars.

CHAPTER 10

"You are behind this!" Taroon shouted at Drenna. "You did this! I'm supposed to think he's kidnapped, and you're hiding him."

"Your father did this, you fool!" Drenna shouted back. "You only pretended to go along with Leed's decision!"

"That makes no sense at all," Taroon said scornfully. "Leed was headed back to Rutan. Why would my father kidnap him?"

"Because it was too late to change the plan. I don't know! All I know is that Leed is gone." Drenna suddenly slumped on the deck. She did not weep, but she rubbed her hands up and down her arms compulsively. "My brother is gone."

Was Drenna's emotion genuine? Obi-Wan looked at Qui-Gon for a clue. He found himself adrift on this mission in more ways than one. He was not sure what anyone was feeling. He was not sure if anyone was telling the truth. But he was sorry to see that the truce between Drenna and Taroon had ended. Now they hated each other more than ever.

Qui-Gon crouched by Drenna's side. "He was kidnapped by Senalis, Drenna," he said gently. "He won't be harmed."

"How can you know this for sure?" she whispered. "What if Rutanians took him back to their planet? What if he gets thrown in jail?"

"I don't know anything for sure," Qui-Gon admitted. "But I do feel that Leed is safe, for the moment. The question is, why would Senalis kidnap him?"

"I don't know," Drenna said, shaking her head. "Leed's decision has split many Senalis. Most believe he should remain, if he wishes. But there are some who do not want a Rutanian to live permanently on the planet."

"We must contact my father at once," Taroon insisted. "He must know that Leed has been taken."

"Yes, he must know," Qui-Gon agreed. "But it would be better if we waited. If we investigate, we might turn up some clues. When we give him the news, we can give him hope as well."

Taroon was already shaking his head. "He must be told now."

"But he could declare war!" Drenna cried.

"That was the risk the Senalis took when they abducted him," Taroon countered. "I was a fool to trust any of you!" He threw a bitter glance at Drenna.

"And I was a fool to think you could have a heart," she replied, just as bitterly.

Taroon stalked off. Qui-Gon turned to Obi-Wan with a sigh.

"We have no choice," he said in a low tone. "We must contact King Frane immediately. If we don't, Taroon will, and our trust with the king will be violated."

He activated his holocom and was put through to the king at once. The king shimmered in the dark night, a ghostly blue presence. Briefly, Qui-Gon told him the news.

"Who took him?" King Frane roared.

"We do not know yet," Qui-Gon answered. "But we will. I can give you my assurance that we will not sleep until we find your son."

"I think you've got enough sleep!" King Frane thundered. "While you fools were dreaming, they stole him from right under your noses! How could you let this happen? You are Jedi!"

Obi-Wan admired again how Qui-Gon could meet insults with composure.

"Jedi are not infallible, King Frane," his Master said evenly. "We are living beings, not machines. I will find your son."

"You'd better," King Frane responded. "Where is Taroon?"

Taroon reappeared out of the darkness. "Here, Father."

"Start for Rutan at once," King Frane ordered. "I do not want you taken as a prisoner of war."

"War?" Qui-Gon asked.

King Frane was grim. "If you don't find my son within the next twelve hours, my army will invade Senali, and we will find him ourselves!"

CHAPTER 11

Taroon gathered his pack hastily, grabbing his items and stuffing them inside.

"You'll need a guide," Qui-Gon said. "Perhaps Drenna will lead you back."

"I do not need a guide," Taroon said angrily. "She will lead me astray and leave me to die, no doubt."

Drenna fixed him with her cool silver gaze. "Don't be a fool. If you go alone, you'll get lost. If you wait until daybreak, the Nali-Erun will lead you to the road."

"That is more time than I want to spend on this vile planet," Taroon said. "Every minute I am here is torture."

Drenna shrugged. "Then swim to shore and find your way through the swamp. Drown or get lost. I don't care."

He glared at her, but she ignored him. Finally Taroon stomped off. He sat down on the dock at a distance from them, facing the horizon where the sun would soon appear.

Qui-Gon motioned to Obi-Wan. "We must contact Meenon and tell him that King Frane is threatening to invade."

Obi-Wan nodded. "I hope he does not insult you the way King Frane did."

Qui-Gon's blue gaze was clear. "King Frane wraps his fear in insults. But what he said was true, Padawan. I should have been more alert. I had not thought it necessary to stay awake, or to trade shifts with you. I had not felt even a trickle of apprehension or danger."

"I did not, either," Obi-Wan admitted. "We were both wrong."

"Then we must accept the consequences," Qui-Gon said. "Now, let us face Meenon."

Qui-Gon activated the holocom. He imagined that Meenon would have to be awakened, but the Senali leader appeared immediately.

"You do not need to tell me your news," he said heavily. "King Frane has threatened invasion. You should be aware that if this occurs, he will bring catastrophe to the entire planet of Rutan. Senalis will no longer allow themselves to be ground under the boot of Rutanian forces. All Senalis will fight, just as we did in the great war. And we will triumph once again."

Meenon's harsh words were choked with anger. The wavering image was faint but conveyed every nuance of his expression.

"Many lives were lost in that war," Qui-Gon said. "It left a devastated planet behind. It took generations before Senali recovered."

"Yet we would fight again!" Meenon cried. "We will not stand for invasion!"

"I think calm is called for, as hard as it is to find it," Qui-Gon said. "Neither Senali nor Rutan wants a war —"

Meenon held up a hand. "Stop. You don't understand. King Frane has imprisoned my daughter, Yaana. The beloved daughter I entrusted to his care. He has thrown her in a filthy prison with criminals. He shall pay."

This was bad news indeed. Qui-Gon had feared it. Each step King Frane took was leading his planet into war. He did not seem to care.

"I do not want a war, it's true," Meenon continued. "But only a foolish ruler would not be prepared to fight. My troops are being mobilized. We will meet their boot with our own force. We will not wait to be invaded. We will invade *them*!"

"I respect your anger and grief," Qui-Gon said carefully. "But if there was a way to free your daughter and avert a war, would you take it? And, if you invade, how do you know that King Frane will not give the order to execute your daughter?"

Meenon hesitated. "I am not a bloodthirsty savage like King Frane," he said at last. "Of course I would try to avert a war. I do not want to see the daughters and sons of Senali killed."

"Then let us find Leed and free Yaana," Qui-Gon urged. "Give us twelve hours. And help us. Tell us if there is some faction, some clan on Senali who could have done this. We saw them in the moonlight. Their skin was smeared with clay, and they wore headpieces of white coral —"

"The Ghost Ones," Meenon interrupted. "I can't say for sure, but it could be. They call themselves a clan but they have no ties of blood. We are not sure who they are. They have appeared only recently. They make trouble between clans. They are against the trade of royal children, of any contact whatsoever with Rutan. I do not know what they want to gain, but it could be the Ghost Ones who took Leed."

"Do you know where they are?" Qui-Gon asked.

He shook his head. "They are nomadic. They have no single camp. You need a good tracker, one who can track over water."

"You must find us one immediately and send the tracker here," Qui-Gon urged.

"But you are with the best right now," Meenon said. "Drenna."

Meenon cut the transmission. Qui-Gon turned to search for Drenna. Taroon sat as far away as he could get from them.

The rest of the deck was empty. Drenna was gone.

"Where did she go?" Obi-Wan breathed. He had not heard her make a sound.

Taroon saw the Jedi searching the deck. He stood and rushed over to them.

"Now do you believe me?" he demanded. "She slipped away when you were busy and my back was turned. She is behind the taking of Leed. She's gone to meet him!"

Qui-Gon scanned the dark lagoon. The dark purple sky was graying. On the horizon a faint line of light told him the sun was rising. He could smell the morning.

Far across the lagoon he saw a tiny ripple of movement. It could have been a fish, but he knew it wasn't. Drenna was swimming. She was almost out of the lagoon, into the open sea.

Taroon followed his gaze. "After her!"

Drenna's firm stroke slowed. She dove underneath the surface. When she reappeared, she changed direction slightly.

"She has gone after them, it's true," Qui-Gon said. "But not because she's one of them. She's gone to track them." He turned to Obi-Wan. "Put on your breather. We must catch her."

"I am coming with you," Taroon said.

"No. You could not keep up with us, Taroon. And your father wants you back on Rutan." Qui-Gon put his hand on Taroon's shoulder. "I know you want to find your brother. But you must trust us. Go back to Rutan. Do not aggravate your father. The worlds are too close to war. We will bring Leed safely to you."

Reluctantly, Taroon nodded. He watched as Qui-Gon and Obi-Wan donned their breathing devices and dove into the lagoon.

The water was chilly, but as they swam their muscles warmed. Every so often Qui-Gon would surface in order to scan for Drenna ahead of them. She was moving at an erratic pace, swimming quickly, diving, and sometimes changing direction. Every few meters she would dive again.

They caught up to her at last. She was underwater, swimming slowly along the lagoon bottom. When she saw them, she pointed overhead and began to shoot toward the surface.

Qui-Gon and Obi-Wan followed. The sun was now visible on the horizon and painted the lagoon with a faint blush of pink light.

"How are you tracking them?" Qui-Gon asked. "Can we help?"

"The rocshore fish," she said. "When a boat passes overhead it blocks out light. The rocshores are very shy and bury themselves in the sand for some time afterward. That's why you can't hunt rocshores on boats. We are lucky the night was so bright. I'm following the mounds. They're hard to see if you don't know where to look. Just follow me."

They dove under the surface again. Drenna swam along the bottom, her head swiveling to take in the sandy surface. Every so often she would come up for air and point in a slightly different direction. Obi-Wan had no idea what had triggered her movement. He found it difficult to see the mounds at all. Was Drenna leading them astray deliberately while the kidnappers got away?

There were so many times on missions that he did not know whom to trust. Qui-Gon seemed to have the gift to see beyond the surface into feelings and motivations that Obi-Wan missed. Qui-Gon never seemed to make a mistake. Only with his former apprentice, Xanatos, had he extended trust too far and met disaster. Xanatos was dead now. Obi-Wan imagined that one such miscalculation was enough for one lifetime. If he watched and learned from Qui-Gon, maybe he could avoid mistakes such as that in the future. Already his past experiences had made him more cautious than he'd been as a student. He was certain he had become a better Padawan as a result.

Drenna wound through the cluster of islands. Sometimes she had to backtrack, but Obi-Wan could see they were making steady progress. He was tiring, but he knew he had reserves of strength he had not yet tapped.

At last she signaled to them to come to the surface with her. A small island was a short distance away, and she jerked her chin toward it.

"I think they are on that island," she whispered. "They dragged the boat up on that beach. They tried to cover the marks, but I can tell by the surface of the sand that it's been swept with fronds. I say we circle around and go ashore."

Qui-Gon scanned the island. "They are most likely in the center of the island, hidden by the trees."

Drenna nodded. "If we're lucky, they haven't posted lookouts. They probably think they are safe. This island cluster is uninhabited. There aren't any clans for many kilometers."

"We'll have to risk going ashore," Qui-Gon agreed. "Don't surface until we're near land. We will follow you."

Taking a deep breath, Drenna disappeared silently under the surface.

Obi-Wan followed Drenna with a new burst of energy. They were close now. If they could rescue Leed and return him to Rutan, war could be averted.

They surfaced silently and waded ashore, quickly dashing across the exposed beach to gain shelter under the branches of the sand-sweeping trees.

"It's a small island," Qui-Gon said quietly. "We won't have to search long before we find them."

Jedi learned early at the Temple how to move without sound, but Senalis were just as practiced at the art. The three of them moved through space without disturbing a leaf. They melted through the shade of the trees, their eyes searching for a telltale clue.

Suddenly Qui-Gon stopped. He held up a hand.

Obi-Wan saw and heard nothing. A stand of trees was ahead, the branches so thick the sun only penetrated in thin, watery fingers of light.

Qui-Gon pointed above, a finger to his lips.

It took Obi-Wan a few seconds to realize that the Senalis were sleeping over their heads, nestled into the thick branches of the trees. Preparing for the dawn raid must have kept them awake throughout the night. Their boat and supplies were suspended in a net high above the ground.

Leed was tied to a tree branch, his back against the trunk. His eyes were closed. His hands and feet were bound with cable wire. A leather gag was tied over his mouth. A deep reddish bruise was forming on his cheekbone. Dried blood caked his tunic.

Drenna didn't flinch. Her jaw tightened, and she silently withdrew the crossbow that was strapped to her back. Qui-Gon withdrew his lightsaber. Obi-Wan followed suit.

Qui-Gon indicated with a gesture that they should try to free Leed without awakening his captors. Obi-Wan and Drenna nodded.

They made no sound as they moved forward, but one of the kidnappers awoke. They froze, but he casually looked down as he stretched. He stopped in the middle of a yawn, his eyes wide.

"Invasion! To your weapons!" he shouted.

CHAPTER 12

The Senalis were armed with the common weapon of their world, dart shooters. Qui-Gon guessed that the darts contained a paralyzing agent. Leed might have some paralysis once they managed to free him.

The darts rained down on them from above. Qui-Gon and Obi-Wan kept their backs to each other in order to cover a complete circle. Their lightsabers whirled above their heads in a blur of blue and green as they deflected dart after dart, even as they made their steady way toward Leed.

The branches of the trees were thickly clustered. The tree where Leed was held would not be difficult to climb. But could they climb, deflect darts, and get Leed down the tree, all at the same time? It would be a challenge, Obi-Wan thought grimly.

"We need to get them down here," Qui-Gon said to him tersely. "If we can fight them on the ground, Drenna can rescue Leed."

"I'll get them down," Drenna said. She hoisted her crossbow to her shoulder and began to fire a rapid volley of laser arrows into the trees. She was a blur of motion, firing off five arrows at a time and barely pausing to reload before firing again. The kidnappers began to drop from the trees to escape the arrows falling on their heads.

"Cover me," she called to Qui-Gon and Obi-Wan, and started for Leed.

The enemy was now all around them, and Qui-Gon and Obi-Wan kept up a constant dance of movement, deflecting the poison darts and keeping the Senalis away from Drenna as she swiftly made her way up the tree. She removed a small fusioncutter from her utility belt and carefully cut away the carbon wire binding Leed's wrists and ankles. He slumped against her, but when she helped him to his feet he was able make his way down the branch toward the trunk. His legs seemed stiff, but he could walk.

Qui-Gon drifted closer to Obi-Wan. "Gather them underneath that tree," he said, indicating one close to them.

Working together, they whirled and attacked, driving the Senalis together as they evaded the darts. They managed to get them in a rough circle where Qui-Gon had indicated.

Qui-Gon leaped into the air and grabbed a high branch. As he swung, he aimed his lightsaber at the net holding the boat aloft. With a series of rapid cuts he sliced through the thick netting. The boat, along with supplies, began to tip. With a final thrust he cut the last cords, and the boat crashed to the ground below.

The kidnappers saw it coming and dropped flat to the ground. The boat reversed in the air and fell over them, forming a solid cage. Supplies rained down on the boat — food, breathing tubes, utility packs, and medpacs.

"Stay under there or we'll blast you," Drenna warned in a loud voice. She raised an eyebrow at Qui-Gon.

He jerked his head toward the beach, and they took off. Most likely the kidnappers would be afraid to follow — at least for a while.

Qui-Gon and Obi-Wan supported Leed as they ran to the shoreline. They dove into the warm sea. Leed gained strength as he swam, with Drenna helping him along.

Drenna pointed to land in the distance. "There," she said. "That's the mainland. We can get to a main road from there."

They struck out toward land. Leed flagged as they got nearer, and Obi-Wan and Qui-Gon had to tow him ashore. He collapsed on the sand and took deep breaths.

"Thank you," he said when he could speak. "I could not have escaped on my own." He gave them a weak smile. "As I'm sure you can see."

"Do you know who the kidnappers were?" Qui-Gon asked.

He shook his head. "They did not speak. They would not answer my questions. I don't know why they took me, or what they were planning to do."

"I am glad you're safe," Drenna told him, gazing at him anxiously. "But you're so weak."

"It's the paralyzing dart," he said. "I'll be better soon."

"We must get to a main road and find a way back to the main city and our transport," Qui-Gon said. He turned to Leed. "Your father is threatening to invade Senali. He means it this time, I fear."

"Taroon is furious," Drenna put in, her eyes flashing. "He thinks you and I arranged the kidnapping. No doubt he will tell his father this."

Leed's eyes were clear. "I must return," he said.

"We are close to a road that often runs supplies to the city," Drenna told the Jedi. "We can hitch a ride from a passing transport."

"Then let's go," Qui-Gon said.

Luck was with them. They flagged down a transport, and the driver quickly agreed to take them back to the floating city. There, they hurried to the Jedi's starship. Leaving word for Meenon that Leed was safe, they took off for Rutan.

"I'm glad you are coming with me," Leed told Drenna. "This won't be a pleasant trip."

"I wouldn't let you go alone," Drenna said gently. "You need care."

"I'd better contact your father," Qui-Gon told Leed. "There's no time to lose." Quickly, he accessed the comm unit and contacted King Frane. He told him that they were on their way to Rutan.

"I'll believe it when I face him on his own royal land," King Frane said, brusquely cutting the connection.

"So much for thank-yous," Obi-Wan muttered.

"He is still worried about his son," Qui-Gon said gently. "He hides his fear well."

"He hides his manners better," Obi-Wan replied.

They landed the craft on the palace grounds and made their way to see the king. He was pacing anxiously outside the Great Hall. When he saw Leed, his forbidding expression gave way to one of delight.

"Ha! I was afraid something would go wrong!

My son, my son!" King Frane hurried forward and hugged Leed. He let him go and mopped at his streaming eyes with the edge of his tunic. "How I missed you. Thank the stars you have come home."

"I came home to talk to you, Father," Leed said. "Not to stay."

Instantly, King Frane's face grew red. "Not to stay?" he shouted. "That's impossible! You are here. You will stay!"

"Father, can we talk without shouting?" Leed asked.

"I am not shouting!" King Frane bellowed. Then he lowered his voice. "It's just that I must speak up, because apparently nobody listens to me."

"I have listened to everything you and Taroon have said," Leed responded steadily. "I have tried to find a way to do my duty. But Father, I know that if I return it will break my heart. I can't rule this world — I don't know it. I don't love it the way I love Senali. You sent me there and made sure I was taken care of. You succeeded. I made a new family there. I belong there. But I assure you I don't mean to be a stranger to my blood family or to Rutan. Senali is close —"

"It's close, but who wants to go there?" King Frane said furiously. "Obviously, you have been swayed by forces on Senali. I'm sure if you

spend time on Rutan you will forget these foolish ideas."

"I will not forget them," Leed said, exasper-
ated. "They are part of me."

King Frane visibly calmed himself, dropping
his hands to his sides and taking a breath.
"Leed, I must speak to you as a king as well as
a father," he said in a voice that struggled to be
steady. "I do not want to bully you into doing
your duty. That is an option that is open to me
as king. But as your father I prefer a more rea-
soned way. You will break my heart if you do
this. You will kill my love for you."

"This is your way of reason?" Leed asked in
astonishment.

"Hear me," King Frane said, holding up a
hand. "Our family line has ruled for a hundred
years. The firstborn child of the king or queen
has taken his or her place without fail. Do you
realize what you do when you break that chain?
Do you take your responsibility to your family
and your world so lightly? How can you decide
at this young age what is right for the rest of
your life?"

King Frane's words struck Obi-Wan as none
had before. When he'd left the Jedi, he had not
fully realized that he'd not only broken a bond
between himself and Qui-Gon, but had violated
a deep tradition between all Masters and Pada-

wans. He had come to see how important his place in that tradition was.

Should Leed return to Senali and turn his back on generations who had prepared the way for him? Suddenly, Obi-Wan wasn't sure.

"You expect me to rule a year from now," Leed countered. "I will have to make such important decisions for all Rutanians. If you trust me to do that, you should trust my own mind now."

King Frane's temper grew, no matter how he tried to suppress it. "You turn your back on those Rutanians you speak of so lightly."

"No," Leed said firmly. "I cannot be a good ruler. This I know. So I turn the honor aside to one more worthy."

"Your brother?" King Frane asked in disbelief. "Taroon is soft. He has no head for leadership. Who would follow him? As soon as he was picked up from that awful planet, I sent him back to school, where he belongs."

"You do not give him a chance," Leed said.

"I don't have to!" King Frane said, his voice rising again. "I am king! I choose! And I choose my firstborn, as my mother chose me, as my grandfather chose her!"

Leed did not answer. His mouth set stubbornly.

King Frane did not speak for a moment.

Father and son faced each other. Neither flinched.

Obi-Wan glanced at Qui-Gon, but as usual the Jedi gave no clue as to what he was thinking. He was merely waiting for the situation to resolve itself as it would. He was so calm! Obi-Wan could feel the tension coiling inside him. He sought for the Jedi composure and could not find it. He could only find confusion.

At last King Frane spoke. "This discussion is over," he said stiffly. "I will not accept disloyalty and betrayal. You must take up your legacy. My son must rule after me. I am doing what is right for you."

"You can't make me do this," Leed said firmly.

King Frane's laughter had a harsh sound. Obi-Wan tried to listen as Qui-Gon would. He realized that the laughter was fueled by bewilderment and hurt, not contempt. "Of course I can! I am king!"

"What about Yaana?" Qui-Gon spoke up. "We have brought Leed to you. Now you must deliver your part of the bargain and free her."

"I made no bargain," King Frane said, his eyes glinting dangerously.

"But you did," Qui-Gon said steadily.

"Well, perhaps I did, but I am breaking it," King Frane said, watching Qui-Gon warily.

"Yaana stays in custody until Leed agrees to begin royal training."

"So that is how you'll force me!" Leed cried. "You'll hold an innocent girl hostage! You are no better than a bully!"

King Frane's expression instantly changed to rage. "Yes, I will do this," he bellowed furiously. "Have you not been listening, you fool? I am king! I can do what I want. I know what is best for Rutan!"

King Frane stalked off, followed by his cluster of advisors and guards. Leed gazed after him, a look of disgust on his face.

"You see why I did not want to return?" he said. "He has found a way to keep me here against my will."

"So it appears," Qui-Gon said neutrally.

"What do you mean?" Drenna asked.

"If we return Yaana to her father, King Frane has nothing to bargain with. He will have to face Leed as father to son, not king to subject."

"But she's in prison," Drenna objected.

"That is the difficulty," Qui-Gon agreed.

"Not necessarily," Leed said slowly. "I think I know how to break her out."

CHAPTER 13

"I'll explain on the way," Leed said. "I know where Yaana is being held. Can we take your transport?"

Qui-Gon nodded. "Let's go."

"Are you sure we should be doing this?" Obi-Wan murmured to Qui-Gon as Leed and Drenna hurried ahead. "We're not supposed to break the laws of a planet."

"Well, we're with the prince," Qui-Gon observed. "Officially, he's now in royal training. We have his permission."

"But if we help Leed, we'll be taking sides," Obi-Wan pointed out.

"No, we're rescuing a hostage," Qui-Gon corrected. "King Frane has no right to hold Yaana in prison. She's only ten years old."

Obi-Wan fell silent. There were times when he had to struggle with Qui-Gon's decisions. His caution would lead him to choose a different way. But it was at such times that he was learning to let go and trust his Master. He knew that it was unjust to hold the girl.

"Don't worry, Padawan," Qui-Gon told him. "I am beginning to see how this situation can be resolved." He smiled. "We just have to break someone out of prison first."

"That's all?" Obi-Wan said. He returned Qui-Gon's smile. Whenever they got out of rhythm, Qui-Gon managed to get them together again, either with a small joke or a gentle correction.

Obi-Wan jumped into the pilot seat of the starship. On Leed's direction, he punched in the coordinates for the landing platform on the outskirts of the city, close to the prison.

"So tell us why you think you have a way to rescue Yaana," Qui-Gon said to Leed as soon as they were under way.

"It was last summer on my visit," Leed began. "I was already trying to tell my father that I preferred Senali to Rutan. Of course he wouldn't listen. There was a grand hunt that day, and I refused to participate. So he threw me in prison."

Qui-Gon looked at him, startled. Drenna gasped.

Leed gave a faint smile. "Just for a day. He said it was for my royal training. So that I would know how Rutan treated its prisoners. It wasn't too bad. Of course everyone knew who I was, so I was given the best cell and no one mistreated me. But an interesting thing happened while I was there. A bird got into the exhaust system and began to fly around the place. It kept tripping the sensors. The guards could not seem to catch it or shoot it, and the sensors kept alerting the main system that a massive prison breakout was in progress. It took them awhile to figure out it was the bird — at first they thought the system had been triggered by a prisoner. But every time they checked out a sensor and did a cell check, everything was fine. The problem was that the system calls for an automatic notification to the king's guard when there is trouble at the prison. My father kept getting notification that a major breakout was going on, and then was told that it was nothing. The hunt was disrupted, and he was furious. They finally had to confess a bird was tripping it. He told the prison to turn off the system and catch the bird, or he'd fire every single one of them."

Drenna laughed. "I like the idea of one tiny creature causing all that trouble."

Leed grinned at her. "I would be lying if I said I didn't enjoy it myself. They turned off the system until they caught the bird. Everyone forgot about me — I was in the warden's office, since they were about to release me. That's when I noticed something. When the guards change shifts, they remove their weapons belts if they are leaving and the guards on the new shift buckle on their own weapons belts. They do this in the weapons supply room, which is kept locked. When they shut the system down, the weapons supply room goes into automatic lockdown. That's in case there's a real breakout. They don't want the prisoners to get access to weapons."

Qui-Gon had already reached Leed's conclusion. "So if the system was shut down during a changeover, there would only be a reduced guard staff on duty with no access to additional weapons."

"Three guards per block, to be exact," Leed said, nodding. "It's a flaw in the system. I tried to tell my father upon my return, but . . . well, let's just say he wasn't in the mood to listen."

"I don't understand," Drenna said. "How can we get a bird to invade the system?"

Qui-Gon smiled. "We don't need a bird. I think Leed has an idea."

"When I arrived, they pretended I was a lawbreaker, just as my father wanted," Leed said, leaning forward with his excitement. "I was led to the booking area, then the holding cell. I had to pass at least ten to fifteen sensors during the whole process." Leed looked at Drenna. "Who has the best aim on Senali?"

"You do," she said promptly.

He shook his head, smiling. "Who tied for first place with me last year in the All-World Games?"

"I did," she said with a grin. "Almost beat you, too."

"You'll be our bird," he said. "All you need is this." He handed her a tiny dart shooter. "With some Jedi help, and a bit of bluffing on my part, I think we can bring this off. You can shoot darts at the sensors as you move through the hallways." He reached in a pocket of his tunic and withdrew some darts. They were tiny and made of transparent material. "These will stick in the wall, but no one will be able to see them."

"But how will we all get inside?" Drenna wondered.

Qui-Gon's eyes shone bright. "That's the easy part. We'll get arrested."

Leed split off from them as soon as they landed. He headed toward the prison. He would pretend to do a spot inspection as part of his royal training. King Frane had lost no time in announcing to the Rutanians that the prince had returned and would take up his legacy.

Qui-Gon, Obi-Wan, and Drenna moved through the crowded streets of Testa. The buildings were carved of enormous blocks of stone in somber colors. The city had a teeming population, and in an effort to retain order there were strict controls on behavior. Qui-Gon felt it would be an easy task to get arrested. He had insisted on avoiding any violence or destruction of property. Instead, they merely needed to find an open park or plaza.

Drenna pointed ahead. "I see a place."

They made sure a pair of security police were nearby as they strolled through a plaza planted with green grass and shrubs. Qui-Gon and Obi-Wan casually unfurled their survival tent and began to set up a condenser unit. Drenna unpacked some food.

Within minutes, the two security police appeared.

"What do you think you're doing?"

"Cooking," Drenna said brightly.

"Loitering is against the law," one of them said. "So is cooking outdoors. Move along."

"But we're hungry," Obi-Wan said.

"We won't be long," Drenna said.

Apparently Drenna's youth and winning smile had an effect. The tall Rutanian policeman looked at his companion, a female even taller than he was. They both shrugged.

"End of my shift," the male murmured.

"I'm too tired for this," the female said. "If we arrest them, I won't be home for dinner."

"We didn't see you, okay?" the first one said, and turned away. "Just pack up and get lost."

The Jedi and Drenna exchanged surprised glances. They had thought this would be the *easy* part of their plan.

"We're staying," Drenna insisted quickly.

"And we're going to feed everyone in the park!" Obi-Wan added. "We brought plenty of food. We can stay until sunset."

Slowly, the two officers turned back.

The female sighed. "Are you going to make this hard or easy?"

Qui-Gon concentrated on her mind. "I guess you have to arrest us."

"I guess we have to arrest you," the officer said. "Stand up."

"Whew," Drenna said under her breath as she leaped to her feet. "I never thought I'd feel relieved to hear that."

They packed up their survival gear under the watchful eyes of the police. They were searched, but Qui-Gon used another Jedi mind trick to prevent the police from confiscating their lightsabers and Drenna's dart shooter, informing them to let them pass unhindered — a command the officers repeated dutifully. Then they were herded into the police landspeeder and transported to the prison.

As they passed through the gray durasteel

gates, Obi-Wan watched as they slid shut behind them. A system of locks snapped shut in a series of loud clicks. Drenna swallowed.

"Are we sure this is a good idea?" she asked.

"It's too late now," Obi-Wan murmured.

"That's exactly what I mean," she said.

CHAPTER 14

Once they got to the prison, they were marched to a booking desk.

"Charge?" the desk clerk asked the two security police.

"Loitering," the tall female said. "Can we do this one quickly, Neece? It's the end of our shift."

The guard looked at his timepiece. "Almost the end of mine, too. Long day. Names?"

Qui-Gon, Obi-Wan, and Drenna gave their names. They were subjected to a retinal scan. The security police left and two guards were called.

"Escort the prisoners to the holding cell."

The clerk activated the security door and they marched through. The door clanged behind them and the locks snapped in with a final sound.

They headed down the hall between the

guards. They had to pass through a number of checkpoints. The sensors glowed red over the open doorways. When the guards approached, they shot at the sensor with a laser pointer located at the tip of an electro-jabber. They were expert at timing their pace with the swing of the jabber in order to make it through the checkpoint smoothly.

The guard on the left swung up his jabber and shot a beam of light at the sensor. It glowed green, but Drenna pretended to cough and brought her dart shooter to her mouth.

Her aim was perfect. The sensor went into a flashing mode, and an alarm sounded.

The guards looked around in surprise. The hallway was empty. The guard's comlink buzzed.

"Guard seven, report in."

He spoke into the comlink. "Nothing here. Must be a malfunction. Check the system."

They continued walking. At the next sensor, Drenna set off the alarm before the guard could raise his jabber. The alarm sounded again.

"Guard seven, report in." This time the voice was annoyed.

"Again, it's nothing."

A groan came over the comlink. "Not another bird."

They passed through four sensors on the way to the holding cell. Drenna was so good at concealing the dart shooter that Qui-Gon did not even have to use the Force. The sensors went off, the alarm clanging.

The guards were clearly annoyed as they ushered the group into the holding cell. They led Drenna and the Jedi in and closed the durasteel door.

"Two minutes to shift change," Qui-Gon said softly.

Drenna put her eye to the small opening in the door. It was just big enough for her to aim the dart shooter. She aimed at the sensor across the hall.

The alarm clanged again.

"Why don't they shut it all down?" the guard outside complained, putting his hands over his ears. "All we need is to get the royal guard down here to investigate."

"Prince Leed is here," the other said. "The king will find out about this no matter what."

"Be quiet," the other muttered. "Here comes the warden. Let's head for our shift change before he tells us we have to stay."

They heard the guards' footsteps receding and then, Leed's voice.

"I don't understand this," Leed said angrily. "Your system must be too sensitive. This has happened before. My father will be furious."

"Yes," the warden said nervously. "Perhaps

another bird, or some sort of small creature, is triggering the system."

"It must be shut down at once!" Leed thundered, sounding like his father.

"But —"

"At once!"

The warden and Leed hurried away. Qui-Gon kept his eye on his timepiece, Obi-Wan on the sensor.

"The sensor just went off," Obi-Wan said. "The system has been shut down."

"And the guards are changing shifts. Time to go." Qui-Gon activated his lightsaber. Obi-Wan followed. Quickly, they cut a hole in the durasteel door. Then the three of them climbed through.

The hallway was empty, but it wouldn't be for long. They raced down the hall. Leed had told them the location of the high security cell where Yaana would most likely be held.

The system was off, but there was now a guard outside Yaana's cell. His blaster was in his holster. No doubt he was not nervous about a ten-year-old girl making an escape attempt.

Drenna blew a paralyzing dart at the guard. It landed in his neck. He toppled over, a surprised look on his face.

Drenna leaned over. "You'll be able to move in twenty minutes," she told him in a friendly way. "Just relax and enjoy the chance to rest."

Meanwhile, Obi-Wan and Qui-Gon swiftly cut a hole in the door. The metal peeled back, and they climbed inside. A slender Senali girl with large dark eyes sat in a corner. She shrank back when she saw the Jedi.

"Yaana, don't be afraid. We have come to take you back to your father on Senali," Qui-Gon told her.

The apprehensive look faded. She raised her chin and nodded. "I am ready."

They ran down the hall. When they reached a turning, Qui-Gon held up a hand. He peered around the corner. Leed was shouting at the warden in a good imitation of his father. When he saw Qui-Gon, he quickly swiveled the warden around by the shoulder so that he would not see them. He made a quick hand motion behind the warden's back to indicate a door near him.

Qui-Gon, Obi-Wan, Drenna, and Yaana moved silently down the hall. Qui-Gon walked to the doorway that Leed had indicated. It led to another long gray hall. This one was lined with closed office doors. They were now in the administrative section of the prison.

A console desk was directly ahead of them. It was the checkpoint to leave the prison. Qui-Gon strode forward.

"We are authorized visitors with an exit pass

signed by the warden," he said. He concentrated on the guard's mind. "We may go."

"You may go," the guard said, activating the door.

Walking casually, the four strolled past the checkpoint and out the door. They quickened their pace as they passed through the yard. When they hit the streets of Testa, Drenna began to hurry, but Qui-Gon stopped her.

"Do not attract attention," he said.

They were almost to the platform when Leed caught up to them.

"So far, so good," he said. "But I'm afraid the warden put in a call to my father to apologize for the disturbance when it first started. He could be here any minute."

"Now you can hurry," Qui-Gon told Drenna.

They ran down the last section toward the landing platform. Their transport sat waiting. The landing platform was deserted.

Suddenly Obi-Wan sensed danger. *This is a public landing platform. Why is it deserted?* he wondered.

He and Qui-Gon activated their lightsabers in one simultaneous motion. Qui-Gon pushed Yaana toward a stack of container boxes. "Get behind them," he ordered crisply.

In the next split second, blaster fire erupted

from around the corner of a tech shed. The ship was peppered with blasts.

They rushed forward, lightsabers activated. A row of guard droids was emptying weaponry into the transport. Blaster fire hit the fuel tank, and it went up in an explosion.

Qui-Gon, Obi-Wan, Drenna, and Leed went after the droids. Drenna's exceptional cross-bow aim sent three of the droids smoking within seconds. Leed fired just as rapidly with his own crossbow, taking down two droids. Obi-Wan and Qui-Gon leaped and tumbled as one unit, lightsabers a blur of motion, to behead the rest.

"Well done," a familiar voice said.

They turned to see King Frane standing with the royal guard. "A pleasure to watch, in fact." He glanced at Drenna with admiration. "I've never seen such good shooting. Who would think a Senali could be such a good shot?"

One of King Frane's nek battle dogs suddenly leaped forward, barking, with its long, deadly teeth bared.

"Back!" the king called to the ferocious dog.

Drenna stepped forward before anyone could stop her. She held out a hand, and the dog quieted, then sniffed her. Qui-Gon had never seen a nek battle dog react in a friendly fashion. By the look on his face, neither had King Frane. Drenna scratched the nek behind the ears.

"You're not a killer. Just misunderstood," she cooed.

"Tell that to a kudana," King Frane said. "Now, where is Meenon's daughter?"

Qui-Gon stepped in front of Yaana, who had emerged from behind the boxes. "We will not let you take her again," he told King Frane. "The Jedi are here at your request. They will not stand by and watch you violate diplomatic law."

King Frane stared him down. "Foolish words. I decide the law on Rutan."

"No, Father." Leed stepped forward. "There is no need to threaten my friends the Jedi. I see I have no choice. I will stay on Rutan."

"At last you see your duty," King Frane said, satisfied.

"Are you sure, Leed?" Qui-Gon asked. "I promised you that we would not allow your father to force you to remain here."

Leed shook his head. "I am not forced. I see now that my legacy is a burden I must accept. Not to do so would be selfish. Perhaps my father was right about that."

"Perhaps?" King Frane asked irritably. "Of course I'm right!"

"And you will allow us to take Yaana back to Senali?" Qui-Gon asked the king.

King Frane shook his head. "Then I will have no Senalis here. I need leverage with Meenon. No. She remains."

"Meenon has set his conditions to avoid war," Qui-Gon said. "One of them is the return of his daughter. I do not think Leed remaining here will change that. Once you threw his daughter in prison, he ceased trusting you."

"Let him attack! What do I care? We will pulverize them!" King Frane cried angrily.

Drenna stepped forward. "Send Yaana home. I will remain."

King Frane looked at her curiously. "And who are you, besides being such a good shot?"

"I am Drenna, Meenon's niece," Drenna said. "I am loved by him, too. If I remain, he will not attack Rutan."

"I am not afraid of his attack," King Frane said scornfully. He eyed her. "Still, it is a solution. All right. I accept."

"You will not imprison her?" Qui-Gon asked warningly.

"No. She will live on the royal grounds, where I can keep an eye on her," King Frane said with satisfaction, turning back to Drenna. "I will install you in the hunting lodge. You'll be under my watchful eye, unable to escape, but not imprisoned. Maybe you will teach my royal guard how to aim. And take care of my neks. Taroon was in charge of care of all my trackers. He was afraid of the neks and never could fix the droids. I'm sure you can't be worse. I will call Taroon from school and send him back to Senali." King Frane stamped his foot. "There, we have a trade once more. Are you satisfied, Jedi?"

"Taroon goes to Senali?" Drenna asked. "But he hates it there!"

King Frane shrugged. "Good. Then I know he will return."

He turned abruptly. "All is over. Now, it's time for the hunt. Come, Leed."

Leed walked closer to Qui-Gon and Obi-Wan. He placed a hand on each of their forearms. Sadness was on his face, but he nodded at them in a dignified way. "I will never forget all you tried to do for me."

"You may call on us again if you need us," Qui-Gon said.

"I am sorry, Leed," Obi-Wan said.

"Duty is more important than feelings," Leed said. "That is what I must learn. I wish you ease and serenity."

He left them to join his father. With a sad glance of good-bye at the Jedi, Drenna joined them. Qui-Gon and Obi-Wan stood watching them go.

"At least Drenna will be here for a time," Obi-Wan observed. "That will give Leed great comfort. The mission hasn't ended as I thought it would. Somehow I thought Leed would be allowed to remain on Senali."

"Is that what you hoped would happen, Padawan?" Qui-Gon asked. "This time you must tell me the truth."

So Qui-Gon had known he had evaded his question back on Senali. "At first I did not want to tell you that I sympathized with Leed," Obi-Wan admitted. "I thought it would remind you of my decision to stay on Melida/Daan and leave the Jedi. I thought it might give you pause about my commitment to you."

"We have put that matter behind us, Padawan," Qui-Gon said. "Do not be afraid to share your feelings with me. I would never hold them against you."

"My feelings seemed to change from day to day," Obi-Wan admitted. "When King Frane spoke to his son, I was moved by his argument, too."

"That is because there is no clear answer," Qui-Gon said. "Emotions are tangled, as I said in the beginning."

"Well, there won't be a war," Obi-Wan said in conclusion. "I'm sorry for Leed. But at least the planets remain peaceful."

"You are wrong, Obi-Wan," Qui-Gon said, his eyes on the king's transport as it rose in the air. "The mission is not over. And I fear the two worlds are closer to war than ever."

CHAPTER 15

Obi-Wan hurried to catch up to Qui-Gon's long stride. The tall Jedi moved purposefully through the crowded streets of Testa.

"But I don't understand," Obi-Wan said. "Why are we close to war? Both leaders got their children back. There is no reason for them to fight."

"It is not them who still wants war," Qui-Gon said. "It was a Rutanian force that kidnapped Leed."

"How do you know?"

"Think back, Padawan," Qui-Gon said as he skirted a food seller. "Was there anything in their camp that could tell you where they came from?"

Obi-Wan focused his mind. He remembered the kidnappers sleeping in the trees. He had immediately assumed they were Senali because of their silvery skin and coral necklaces and headpieces.

Except they didn't have silvery skin. He had just assumed that they did.

"Their skin was smeared with clay," he said. "I thought it was because they wanted to look fierce. But it could conceal the fact that they didn't have tiny scales on their skin."

"Good," Qui-Gon approved. "Anything else?"

Obi-Wan thought back to the battle. The kidnappers had fought well, but there was nothing to indicate whether they were Senali or Rutanians. Both groups used crossbows and dart shooters as weapons.

He turned his attention to the boat. It had looked like many other boats he'd seen on Senali. It was fashioned from the trunk of one of the native trees. He remembered the supplies raining down from it —

"The breathing tubes," he exclaimed. "Senali don't use them. Why didn't I think of that before?"

"We have not had much time for reflection," Qui-Gon said kindly. "I noticed it, but I had already questioned why they had smeared their skin with that white clay."

"But if you knew they were Rutanians, why didn't you say something?" Obi-Wan asked.

"Because I didn't know who was behind the kidnapping yet," Qui-Gon said. "Until I did, I thought it better to seem to think what I was meant to think."

"So who *is* behind it?" Obi-Wan asked, frustrated. "And where are we going now?"

"We are going to see Taroon," Qui-Gon said.

"But he is probably on his way to Senali," Obi-Wan pointed out.

"Not yet. He will find a reason to delay."

Obi-Wan still felt confused. "You think Taroon was behind the kidnapping of his brother? But why? He came to persuade him to return to Rutan for good. He was angry and hurt when Leed refused."

"Or so he seemed. But Padawan, what beings say and what they feel are not necessarily the same. Jedi are different that way."

"Are you afraid that Taroon is planning an attack?" Obi-Wan asked.

Qui-Gon nodded. "I saw something else in the supplies at the kidnappers' camp. Seeker droids. They had the royal crest of Rutan on them. And King Frane just told us that Taroon was keeper of his trackers, remember? Only one person could have had access to those droids and the power to gather supporters for a secret invasion of Senali."

"Why would Taroon steal the royal seeker droids?" Obi-Wan asked. He was growing frustrated.

"That is a very good question, Obi-Wan," Qui-Gon said. "Why, since seeker droids are so readily available? It only makes sense if Taroon modified the droids in some way. Then he planned to send them back to Rutan."

"And what happens then?"

"That is something Taroon must tell us," Qui-Gon answered gravely.

Obi-Wan saw that they had stopped outside the gates of an impressive structure. ROYAL SCHOOL OF LEADERSHIP was carved in stone over the archway.

Qui-Gon strode through the archway and pushed open the door to the school. The hallway was empty except for a teacher hurrying past, his arms filled with datapads and readout screens.

"Excuse me," Qui-Gon said politely. "We are looking for Taroon."

The teacher frowned. "He is on his way to Senali, most likely. His father gave the order to leave immediately. Pity. He is a popular student. He'll be missed."

"We have reason to believe he has not left yet," Qui-Gon said. "Is there anyplace you can think of that he might be?"

"That's easy," the teacher said with a smile.

"Taroon is usually in the tech room with his friends, tinkering with program boards. It's down that hall, up the ramp, second door on the right."

Qui-Gon thanked him and they moved quickly in the direction the teacher had indicated.

"If you're right, what makes you think Taroon will confess to you?" Obi-Wan asked Qui-Gon.

"Because he is not bad," Qui-Gon said. "Merely hurt. He is like his father — he turns his hurt to anger."

They came to the tech room and activated the door. Taroon sat on a long bench against the wall. He looked up at the Jedi nervously and jumped to his feet.

"Has anything happened?" he asked.

"Why do you ask?" Qui-Gon queried.

Taroon shrugged, but his eyes were wary. "I'm surprised to see you here."

"Your father has sent an order for you to leave for Senali immediately," Qui-Gon said. "Why do you remain?"

"I had left some equipment here," Taroon said quickly. "I need to include it in my packing so I can be on my way."

"You weren't packing when we came in," Obi-Wan pointed out.

Taroon gave him a haughty look. "Who are you to question a prince?"

"He is a Jedi," Qui-Gon said firmly. "Your father called us here to help settle this matter. It is not settled, is it, Taroon?"

"I don't know what you mean," the young man said nervously.

"Taroon, we don't have time for evasions," Qui-Gon said. "I think you were behind your brother's kidnapping on Senali."

"That's ridiculous!" Taroon cried. "Why would I arrange such a thing? I love my brother. I am a patriot!"

"Both of those things are true," Qui-Gon said. "You love your brother, but you are also angry at him for turning his back on you. You are a patriot, but you would arrange an attack on Rutan in hopes Leed would be blamed. But Leed is here, Taroon. I doubt the king will blame him. He will blame Meenon. Maybe he will retaliate, and a war will result. But perhaps you don't care about that. Perhaps you think such an event would tear Leed in two. Perhaps you want this."

"I don't know what you're talking about, but I do know there will not be a war," Taroon said. "My father talks and talks, but he will not attack. Anyway, I had nothing to do with any of this."

"You know your father will not attack Senali for sure? You are willing to gamble lives on it?" Qui-Gon questioned, his tone growing in intensity. Obi-Wan did not think he could have withstood such a piercing gaze.

Taroon's glance slid away. "You can't talk to me this way."

Qui-Gon strolled farther into the room. "Let me tell you what I think happened," he said. "You enlisted a small group of Rutanians. Perhaps they are friends of yours at school, a mix of those who are close to you and those who hope to benefit should you become king instead of Leed. While you remained on Rutan, this group secretly traveled to Senali and established a ghostly identity, just enough to alert Meenon of their presence. They smeared themselves with clay so that no one would be able to see that their skin wasn't scaled. They stole things or violated sacred places so that different clans would grow angry with one another. They fostered unrest to gain attention and dislike among Senali. All of this you planned."

Sweat beaded up on Taroon's forehead. "You can't prove anything."

"You arranged to kidnap Leed because during his disappearance you would arrange an attack on Rutan. You wanted him as the leader of the Ghost Ones to be blamed. Even though Leed escaped, you decided to continue with the plan. Evidence will point to Leed as the one who orchestrated the attack. This will serve to banish Leed from Rutan forever — and won't make him terribly popular on Senali, either, as the Ghost Ones will suddenly disappear. The Senalis will blame Leed, too. He will be left with no world at all. No supporters. And you will become king. Isn't that right, Taroon? You betrayed your brother for your own ambition."

"Not ambition! Love for my planet!" Taroon burst out. "Leed is right. He is not the true ruler of Rutan. Doesn't he deserve what will happen? He turned his back on us long ago! He is my brother. He should have thought of his family. He should have thought about me. I grew up without him. I had to withstand the rages of our father. He grew up with care and love. I grew up with neglect!"

"Your father is many things, but you cannot say he does not love his sons," Qui-Gon said gravely. "Perhaps he does not see you as the strong young man you are."

"He does not see me at all," Taroon muttered.

"It must be hard to be called a fool by your father," Qui-Gon said. "Your anger is understandable. But you are feeding your anger instead of seeking to conquer it. If you faced your father and spoke your truth to him, the situation could change. Instead, you strike out like a child. The difference is that you are a prince, and the result of your anger will be war."

"There won't be a war. Just an attack. No lives will be lost," Taroon said sullenly. "I picked a symbolic target."

"How will it occur?" Qui-Gon asked urgently. "Is it the seeker droids?"

Taroon nodded reluctantly. "The squad on Senali is returning to Rutan. They will release the droids. I have already made sure the droids my father will use on the hunt will malfunction. The new droids will take their place and no one will notice."

"And what will the seeker droids do?" Qui-Gon asked.

"Instead of searching out kudana, they have been programmed to hone in on the nek dog kennels. The kennel has no roof and is open to the sky. When the droids locate their prey, they are programmed to blow apart. In a confined space like the kennels, the dogs will be destroyed."

Taroon shifted uncomfortably under their scrutiny. "What is so terrible? The neks are horrible creatures. They attack anything, even their own kind."

"Yes," Qui-Gon said softly. "Attacking one's own kind is truly despicable."

Taroon's blue skin turned an angry red. He understood Qui-Gon's point: that he himself had turned against his brother.

"This attack will be enough to enrage your father," Qui-Gon said. "And he will suspect Leed. If he does not, you will plant the idea in his head. That's why you remain here and do not leave for Senali. But what about Drenna?"

Taroon looked at him sharply. "What about her? She is back on Senali."

Qui-Gon shook his head. "She remained on Rutan. Your father has installed her in the hunting lodge."

Taroon jumped up. "But the lodge is next to the kennels!"

Qui-Gon nodded. "And her job is to take care of the animals. She could be in the kennels right now."

"No!" Taroon cried. "It is too late to bring back the seeker droids! We have to stop them!"

"Yes," Qui-Gon said. "Perhaps we can prevent what you have set in motion."

"We can use my transport," Taroon said. "Follow me."

CHAPTER 16

Taroon sat at the console, leaning forward as if he could force the transport to go faster. Qui-Gon sat still and calm. As always, Obi-Wan admired his Master's ability to locate his own serenity in the middle of a tense situation.

"I'm confused again," Obi-Wan said, leaning closer to Qui-Gon and speaking in a low voice. "I thought Taroon hated Drenna. Why should knowing she is in danger make a difference to him?"

Qui-Gon gave a short smile. "Remember what I told you at the start of the mission, Padawan. Words do not always echo feelings. You saw two enemies. I saw two young beings fighting an attraction they knew was inappropriate."

Obi-Wan shook his head. "I did not see that at all."

"Do not fret," Qui-Gon said serenely. "Perhaps

if you were older, you would have. In any event, there are things you see that I do not. Such is the nature of the effective Master–Padawan team."

"I hope we reach Drenna in time," Obi-Wan said.

"Here we are," Taroon called in a relieved voice. "I don't see anything. Maybe the hunt was called off."

"Just land the ship," Qui-Gon said, his keen eyes searching the area.

Obi-Wan joined him, scanning the horizon in all directions as Taroon flew lower. Obi-Wan saw a flicker of something in the distant sky.

"There," he murmured to Qui-Gon.

"Yes," Qui-Gon said in a low tone. "Set this down quickly, Taroon," he called in a calm tone. Obi-Wan knew he did not want to panic the young man.

"There's Drenna!" Taroon called, momentarily distracted. "She's heading out from the woods."

Drenna strode out from the woods, her crossbow strapped to her back. Obi-Wan quickly glanced at the flickering dots to his left. Now he could see they were unmistakably seeker droids — perhaps a dozen of them. Silently, he pointed them out to Qui-Gon. He knew from experience how quickly those droids could track.

Drenna looked up and saw the transport. She shaded her eyes from the sun, but could not see inside. She headed for the kennels.

"No!" Taroon shouted. The transport wobbled as his hands shook.

Qui-Gon vaulted forward. He took the controls from Taroon and in a series of swift, practiced moves, landed the craft in the field adjoining the kennels. He activated the landing ramp.

"Hurry, Padawan," he urged.

They raced down the ramp, their lightsabers activated and ready.

Drenna was almost to the door of the kennels. The seeker droids flashed as they zoomed toward the target.

"Drenna!" Qui-Gon shouted. "Overhead! Watch out!"

Drenna's reflexes were keen. She turned, already looking overhead. She barely paused to register the threat before sweeping her arm back to bring her crossbow to her shoulder.

Qui-Gon took a dazzling leap into the air, his lightsaber a bright green glow against the gray sky. He smashed at the lowest seeker droid. The lightsaber sailed through it, cutting it in half. A small explosion sent a puff of smoke rising in the air. As long as the seeker droids did not hit the ground, they would not emit a full explosion.

Obi-Wan followed Qui-Gon with his own leap. He could not get the same height as Qui-Gon, and his first swipe met empty air. But Drenna had already loaded her crossbow and let the first laser arrow fly. It connected, and another droid smoked and sizzled as it crashed to the ground.

Qui-Gon leaped up on the low flat roof of the entrance to the kennels. From here he could move from side to side, taking down the droids as they honed in on the kennel. He could hear the dogs snarling in the open kennels as the droids came closer.

Obi-Wan leaped up to join him. Drenna stayed on the ground, her crossbow at her shoulder, firing so fast her arm was a blur as she fitted arrow after arrow against the bow. Obi-Wan leaped and brought a droid down in a sky-to-ground sweep, then reversed direction and brought down another.

The noise of galloping huds came to them, and Obi-Wan saw the king and the royal party racing toward them. He ignored them, returning his attention to the droids overhead. They were relentless machines, honing in on their target.

One by one, the Jedi and Drenna brought down the droids. There was only one left, diving and spinning toward the kennels. They heard a pop, and the droid began to smoke. Taroon had brought it down with a blaster.

The four of them dropped their weapons to their sides. Drenna wiped the sweat off her forehead with the sleeve of her tunic.

"Would you mind telling me what that was about? And what are you doing here?" she asked Taroon.

"I should ask the same question!" King Frane cried, leaping off his hud and stamping toward them. "Why are my droids here instead of tracking kudana? And why did you destroy them?" His fierce eyes raked the Jedi. "I forgave you once. What makes you think I would do so again?"

"I think it's time you explained, Taroon," Qui-Gon said, giving him a meaningful glance.

"I was very angry," Taroon said to his father. "And I thought . . . if Leed throws away what I want so much, why shouldn't I have it? Why should he be forced to take a prize I covet?"

"You want to rule?" King Frane asked, dumbfounded.

"Yes, Father, I want to rule," Taroon said. "Even though I am the younger brother, and clumsy and weak in your eyes. Even though I am not nearly as good at everything as your firstborn. I knew the only way to get what I wanted was to make it happen. So when Leed began to hint that he wanted to stay on Senali, I saw what would happen. I knew he was heading for a clash of wills. I knew he would not break down, that you would underestimate his stubbornness. So I gathered a group of supporters and sent them to Senali to pose as a fringe clan. My plan was that both Rutanians and Senalis would think that Leed led this fringe clan. I planned the attack with the seeker droids so that all would think that Leed was responsible. War would be threatened, but I did not think it would occur. Leed would stay on Senali. That was before the Jedi got involved." Taroon gave a weak smile at Qui-Gon. "They spoiled all my plans."

King Frane stared at his son in disbelief. "You planned to attack your own planet?"

"No lives would be lost," Taroon insisted. "Only nek battle dogs, and they are of no consequence."

"They are living creatures!" Drenna broke in angrily.

"They eat their own kind! They are bred to destroy," Taroon said. "A few less of them won't make a difference."

"Would you destroy any creature to get your own way?" Drenna asked scornfully. "Is that why you almost destroyed me?"

"I am truly sorry for that," Taroon said, turning to her. "The hunting lodge has been uninhabited for fifteen years. I had no idea you were here."

"Your apology would not mean much to me if I were dead," Drenna shot back.

"Will you two stop?" King Frane roared. "I am the injured party here! My kennels were almost destroyed! And you," he said to Taroon. "Do you mean to tell me that you recruited a squad, invaded a planet, and formed a plan to incriminate your brother in order to rule?"

Taroon nodded.

King Frane froze for a moment. Then he tossed back his head and suddenly broke into a shout of laughter. "How do you like that! He is a leader! Such treachery! Such wiles! You will make a fine ruler. Am I not wise, to raise such a son?" He pounded Taroon on the back. "All you lack is a queen who will fight with you every day, as your beloved mother did with me. What a warrior she was!" He eyed Drenna. "Well, perhaps if you are lucky you will find such a queen nearby."

Drenna looked away, her cheeks flaming as her blue skin flushed with pink. Taroon was equally red. Leed looked from one to the other, a look of surprise on his face. Then, slowly, he smiled.

"Perhaps there will someday be a way for

Senalis and Rutanians to be at peace, after all," he said.

"And us, brother?" Taroon asked, turning to Leed. "Are we at peace? Do you forgive me?"

Leed grasped both of Taroon's forearms in a gesture of affection. "I understand and forgive you, brother."

King Frane's eyes misted, and he cleared his throat noisily. "I, too, would like peace. Already I am tired of these threats and counter threats with Meenon. It interferes with hunting and feasting. I say Leed will be the first ambassador for both worlds. He will foster understanding and trade between the two of us."

"That is a wonderful idea, Father," Leed said, joy entering his voice. "And you will allow me to leave Rutan?"

King Frane waved his hand dismissively. "I am also weary of your sighing and your constant sorrow. It has been very depressing to have you around." He beamed at his two sons. "Now I see that I have two sons who are growing to manhood unafraid of taking what they want. I have done well." He turned to the Jedi. "I forgive you for destroying my droids. Again! Am I not generous? And I invite you to my feast."

Qui-Gon bowed. "We would be honored."

*   *   *

The next day, the Jedi took off with Leed in a transport that King Frane insisted on giving them to replace the starship he had destroyed.

The blue-green world of Senali glittered as they flew closer. They landed and walked with Leed back to his home. The Banoosh-Walore clan spilled out of their home and raced toward Leed, crying out their love and welcome. He instantly disappeared in a flurry of hugs and embraces.

"I thought I had already learned what I needed to know about how personal happiness can conflict with duty," Obi-Wan said, watching Leed. "At first I thought Leed should remain here. Then I thought just as strongly that he should return to his own world. And now I feel that he belongs here after all." Obi-Wan sighed. "I spent much of this mission in a state of confusion."

"That is good, Padawan," Qui-Gon said. "It means you are learning."

"When I think about how I left the Jedi order, the memory is so painful," Obi-Wan said slowly. "It's hard not to feel discouraged that I have so much more to learn."

"It should not be cause for discouragement," Qui-Gon said gently. "Life is both learning and relearning. You can confront the same issue over and over, and find a deeper meaning each time. The learning deepens, and that is what nourishes us. You should take comfort in the fact that life will always surprise you. You taught me after Melida/Daan that my own ideas needed to expand. I have my own lessons to learn."

"Well, it is good to hear that you don't know everything," Obi-Wan told his Master with a smile.

"Not nearly, Padawan," Qui-Gon said. "Not nearly enough, I suspect. Even with sureness, there must be doubt. It is the Jedi way."

JEDI APPRENTICE

The Deadly Hunter

"This place doesn't look as if it provides a soft landing to me," Obi-Wan observed, casting a dubious eye at the Soft Landings Inn. "More like a full-scale crash."

"I've seen many places such as this," Qui-Gon said. "It is a place for space travelers to get a few hours of sleep. It's not arranged for comfort."

The building was made from salvaged materials — durasteel sheets and conductor pipes that wrapped around the building as though they were strangling it to a last gasp. The entire structure leaned to one side. It looked as if a small push could knock it over. The stairs leading up to a battered durasteel door were lined with overflowing garbage bins.

"Well," Qui-Gon said philosophically, "we might as well get this over with."

They mounted the stairs and pressed a button to access the door. A voice came from a speaker mounted next to the frame.

"*Na hti vel?*"

"Visiting a guest," Qui-Gon said.

The door slid open. A small Togorian female shuffled out.

"We're looking for a woman," Qui-Gon said. "She's humanoid and wears a plastoid armor plate —"

"Third level. Number two." The Togorian swiveled to return to her room.

"What's her name?"

The Togorian didn't turn. "Who cares? Pays in advance."

Qui-Gon lifted an eyebrow at Obi-Wan. Obviously, the Soft Landings Inn didn't worry about security.

They hurried up the creaking stairs to the third level. Qui-Gon knocked on the door marked 2. There was no answer.

"I am Qui-Gon Jinn, a Jedi Knight," Qui-Gon called through the door. "We mean you no harm. We just wish to ask you some questions. I respectfully request permission to enter."

Again, there was no answer. But after a moment, the door slowly slid open. Obi-Wan sensed a slither of movement near the floor, but no other disturbance. The door seemed to have opened on its own. It was dark inside the room, and he could not see anyone. He felt danger shimmer out at him like cracks in broken transparsteel.

Qui-Gon must have felt the warning as well. Yet he walked boldly into the room without drawing his lightsaber. Obi-Wan did the same.

Qui-Gon headed directly to a window. He tilted the shade and pale yellow light filtered in.

The bounty hunter sat facing them on a stool, her back against the wall. Her shaved head picked up the light and gleamed like a pale moon. Her dark eyes studied her visitors without interest. Underneath the plastoid chest plate and thigh-high boots, her body was powerful and strong. When she stood, she would be close to Qui-Gon's height.

"We come on behalf of Didi Oddo," Qui-Gon said politely. "You are trying to capture him, yet he has done no wrong. He requests that you check your information or contact the government or party that has sent you. He is sure that you have located the wrong person. Will you do this?"

The bounty hunter said nothing. Her eyes stayed on Qui-Gon, but they were expressionless.

"Didi Oddo runs a café," Qui-Gon said. "He is not a criminal. He rarely leaves Coruscant."

Silence.

"If you would allow me to check the warrant, I could clear this up immediately," Qui-Gon said. "Then we could be on our way."

More silence. Obi-Wan forced himself to remain still. He knew better than to fidget. This was a contest of wills. Qui-Gon stood easily, the same polite expression on his face. He would not show the bounty hunter that she had intimidated him with her silence. No one intimidated Qui-Gon.

"I'm afraid I must insist," Qui-Gon said, his voice hardening a fraction. "If a wrong has occurred, we should check it immediately. You would want the same."

Again, the bounty hunter did not reply. She appeared bored by her visitors. Or maybe she slept with her eyes open . . .

The movement came out of nowhere, taking him by surprise. He had been watching her face in order to determine what she would do. She barely moved a muscle, but with a casual flick of her fingers a whip arched into the air, its spiked tip heading straight for his face.

Obi-Wan backed up, but the whip curled around his neck several times. It tightened as he clawed at it.

Qui-Gon's extraordinarily fast reflexes were sharper than his own. His lightsaber activated in a blur of light. He sprang forward to slash at the whip in order to sever it.

But the bounty hunter's agile fingers flicked again, and the whip reversed its twist and uncoiled off Obi-Wan's neck. It was just out of the lightsaber's reach, taunting Qui-Gon's blade.

The bounty hunter sprang to her feet. The whip flashed again, this time wrapping around Obi-Wan's ankles as he stepped forward to attack.

Obi-Wan stumbled and had to break his fall with one hand. Heat blazed in his face. He hated to be clumsy. This was the second time the bounty hunter had surprised him. Fury clouded his vision for a moment, and he had trouble focusing on the calmness he would need for the battle.

The whip retracted. Suddenly, it glowed red in the dim room. It had been turned to laser mode.

Qui-Gon's lightsaber tangled with the whip. Smoke rose as the two lasers buzzed. Even while entangled with the lightsaber, the bounty hunter manipulated the end of the whip so that it slashed at Qui-Gon's forearm. Qui-Gon was forced to retreat and come at his opponent from another direction.

Obi-Wan leaped forward to help him, already

flexing so that he could come at her with a re-
verse backhand sweep. She flipped backward
three times to avoid him, then dropped unex-
pectedly to the floor and rolled in a ball back to
the window. Her movements were liquid, as
though she were boneless. Obi-Wan had never
seen such acrobatic skill.

The window was open a few centimeters at
the bottom. To Obi-Wan's astonishment, the
bounty hunter shed her armor and flattened
herself enough to slip through the small opening like water. In another moment, she was
gone.

Qui-Gon deactivated his lightsaber. He stood
staring after the bounty hunter. "A formidable
opponent."

The Early Adventures of
Obi-Wan Kenobi and Qui-Gon Jinn

STAR WARS®

JEDI APPRENTICE

Visit us at www.scholastic.com